HARDBALL

orca sports

HARDBALL

STEVEN BARWIN

ORCA BOOK PUBLISHERS

Library and Archives Canada Cataloguing in Publication

Barwin, Steven, author
Hardball / Steven Barwin.
(Orca sports)

Issued in print and electronic formats.
ISBN 978-1-4598-0441-8 (pbk.).--ISBN 978-1-4598-0442-5 (pdf).--
ISBN 978-1-4598-0443-2 (epub)

I. Title. II. Series: Orca sports
PS8553.A7836H37 2014   jC813'.54   C2014-901586-0
C2014-901587-9

First published in the United States, 2014
Library of Congress Control Number: 2014935389

Summary: Griffin's intent to win a baseball scholarship is put on hold when he
must prove his cousin innocent of using steroids.

RECYCLED
Paper made from
recycled material
FSC® C103567
www.fsc.org

*Orca Book Publishers is dedicated to preserving the environment and has printed
this book on Forest Stewardship Council® certified paper.*

Orca Book Publishers gratefully acknowledges the support for its publishing
programs provided by the following agencies: the Government of Canada through
the Canada Book Fund and the Canada Council for the Arts, and the Province of
British Columbia through the BC Arts Council and
the Book Publishing Tax Credit.

Cover photography by Corbis Images
Author photo by Jenna Grossi

ORCA BOOK PUBLISHERS
PO Box 5626, Stn. B
Victoria, BC Canada
v8R 6s4

ORCA BOOK PUBLISHERS
PO Box 468
Custer, WA USA
98240-0468

www.orcabook.com
Printed and bound in Canada.

17 16 15 14 • 4 3 2 1

*To my students: continue to stand up
for what you believe in…
even if it goes against the grain.*

Chapter One

A bat hadn't even cracked a ball and Wade was already talking stats, scouts and scholarships.

"Griffin, being seniors means that we're at the top of the food chain." He tucked his black hair under his baseball hat. "This is our year to lead the Sharks to the playoffs."

No matter how many home runs and RBIs I managed to get, he always seemed to find a way to double that. "Go Sharks."

He slapped my back and it stung. "You should be more pumped!"

"I am. I just want to get out there and play shortstop."

"You're the king at setting up double and triple plays."

We moved away from the locker room and onto the field behind the high school. "It's good to be back out here," I said. "This is our season!"

Wade looked at me and smiled, exposing a pink wad of bubble gum. I could see my reflection in his dark sunglasses. "Yeah, it feels great to be back in the South Coast Sharks uniform. How do I look?"

"Black and red are your colors."

"That's what I like to hear. Man, I can't believe we're finally in charge."

"You mean, other than Coach."

Wade pumped his fist into his glove. "When Coach Brigman isn't around, it's my team—our team."

"Yeah, Coach expects us to step up."

"That's what I'm talking about."

"Hey, you remember how my cousin made the cut?"

"I don't care about freshmen. They're expendable."

"His name is Carson. He might be a freshman, but do me a favor and don't give him a hard time."

"You know me." Wade smiled. "I don't like to play favorites."

"That's not what I mean."

We got to the diamond and tossed a ball around in the outfield until the rest of the Sharks showed. Being first sent a message to the others. Carson showed up next, a bundle of skinny energy under bright red hair.

"Calm down," I whispered to him. I had told him to play it cool and try not to speak for the first week or so. Listening is the best way to survive initiation.

"Just excited to play ball!"

I reluctantly introduced him to Wade, and Carson raised his hand for a high five. Wade left him hanging, but Carson took it in stride.

"Nah, that's cool, man." Carson took a bottle of suntan lotion from his back pocket. "Anyone want?"

Wade gave me a look while Carson rubbed lotion all over himself. "I thought this day would never come!" Carson said with a smile.

Coach Brigman arrived with his two assistant coaches as the rest of the team poured onto the field. He examined the team from under the brim of his hat. "Look at the bunch of you," he said in a way that could be taken as a compliment or an insult. He looked over us to the outfield. "Most of you were late. Give me ten laps."

I jumped to it while Carson kept a few strides behind me with the other new players. As I rounded center field, Wade tapped my shoulder.

He pointed over the fence to a small swamp. "Lake Wade."

"Lake Wade," which was home to a few alligators, was where Wade liked to send his home-run balls. Every couple of weeks he'd get a caretaker to try and scoop them up with a leaf skimmer. Assuming, of course, a gator hadn't gotten to them first. As I entered my final lap, the coaches were just finishing setting up for practice.

Coach Brigman called the team in for a huddle. I got down on one knee and coughed loudly to get Carson's attention to do the same. It was a sign of respect.

Brigman introduced McKay as the pitching coach and Santos as the hitting specialist.

"The season doesn't start with the first game. It starts now. Don't wait to give your hundred and ten percent. Do it now. If you want to win, win now. Do you want to win?"

I shouted back with everyone else, "Yes, Coach!"

"Do you want the championship?"

"Yes, Coach!"

The coaches broke us into groups based on our positions. I stayed with Coach Brigman and the infielders. For a drill called the shuffle, Brigman had us drop our gloves and divided us into three lines. He tossed a baseball on the ground to my right, and I shuffled to grab it and toss it back to him. As I started moving back into position, he tossed another baseball to the far left. I scooped it up and returned it, heading right to grab the next one.

"On the balls of your feet and hustle!" yelled Coach Brigman.

After six back-and-forths, I stepped back in line. I did three rotations, enough to break a sweat, and then Brigman switched things up.

"Everyone grab your gloves and team up with someone."

Wade snatched up Carson, so I paired with Darren. He was extremely serious about baseball. When he pulled a hamstring at the end of last season, he managed to memorize the starting lineups on every American League team during his recovery.

"Those the new guys?" Darren asked, pointing at the three freshmen.

"Yeah. The one on the left is my cousin." We started off in pairs, grabbing the ball out of the grass. Darren and I one-bounced the ball back and forth to each other. When we got into a rhythm,

Coach mixed things up by getting us to go faster. Then he moved us farther apart. There were seventeen guys on the team, and everyone was assigned a backup position. I played shortstop, but there had been times where I was called in to cover outfield. These kinds of drills helped everybody, no matter what his position.

After practice, with the coaches out of sight, Wade stood on the wooden bench in the dugout. He walked the length of it, nudging players off the edge with his feet. "This is going to be an awesome year!" He continued down the line. "Sharks are going all the way." Wade got some cheers until he noticed one of the new guys talking to the guy beside him. He crouched down next to him. "What do you think you're doing?"

"Don't say anything," I muttered to myself. Tim or Tom—it started with a *T*—smiled, thinking Wade was joking. But then Wade started really getting into his face. Everyone else took a step back. "I don't know what's so funny. What's your name?" said Wade.

"Tom. I'm sorry."

I knew where this was going, but I didn't want to jump in unless I had to.

"You're a freshie," Wade said. "You don't talk while I'm talking."

Tom stepped back toward me and the rest of the team. Safety in numbers.

"Don't ever look me in the eye." He pointed at Carson, Tom and the other new kid, Adrian. I recognized him from working at the golf club. "That goes for all three of you. If you want respect from your seniors, then you need to earn it."

Wade loved to show off his temper. I knew he was just blowing off steam because he could. I might not have agreed with what he was saying, but I understood how guys who had paid their dues wanted others to as well. No one was getting a free ride.

Wade set some more ground rules. The boys weren't allowed to speak until spoken to. They had to do what Wade said when he said it. And he was just getting started. "School rules are that you have to keep a B average if you want to stay on a team.

So to help you out, you get to do math homework for me, Griffin and Darren."

I could see the boys stifle a moan. Under the brim of his hat, Carson looked at me.

"Got a problem, redhead?" Wade snarled.

Carson shook his head.

"You can do my homework." Wade looked for a reaction from me, but I wasn't going to give him one. It wasn't a battle worth fighting.

"And if any of you squeal to the coach, well, all this will seem like a walk in the park."

I thought back to my first year with the Sharks. It hadn't been easy being the new guy. I remembered being made fun of when I messed up. When I struck out with the go-ahead run on third, a senior had made me his personal butler. I'd had to get his lunch, wait for him to finish and then clean up after him. The guy ate like a pig on purpose. Three weeks later, at bat in the same situation, I'd made sure to lean into the pitch. Getting hit by the ball was a guaranteed walk, and I didn't have to play butler again.

"We good?" Wade asked Darren and me.

We both nodded. I could live with what he was doing considering I'd expected a lot worse. Then again, the season was young. Who could say how far Wade would take things?

Chapter Two

I held out my hand to receive a George Washington from an old guy in a yellow golf shirt. His clubs were hoisted over my shoulder, ready for the storage shed. It wasn't a fun job, but because I hated serving food, and working in the kitchen was worse, being a bag-drop attendant was my only option. "How was your game, sir?"

"One of my best."

"Glad to hear it." I put the money in my pocket. Or, as I liked to call it, my college fund. I cleaned his clubs and then drove the cart around the corner for charging. As I carried his clubs into the members' storage shed, I spotted Wade.

He looked up, his hand deep inside a golf bag. "Oh, it's only you."

"Find anything interesting?"

"Five bucks and change."

I'd warned Wade that he could be fired for going through people's bags, but he always said he could easily move on to another golf club. He's probably right. I've worked at two others, and there isn't much difference. The members are the same. Rich folks who keep their eyes on the Cuban gardeners while we keep ours on the pretty granddaughters. I'd fallen for one or two over the years. Wade plucked them like they were oranges dangling off trees. He'd offer to show them *the real Florida*, not the kind they'd see in the confines of these gates or the discount-shopping malls.

We walked back to the bag drop-off stand. "Can't wait to kill at the season opener tomorrow," Wade said. "We're going to get scouted, win scholarships to U of Miami and play for the Hurricanes."

Wade and I high-fived, and then we each took a scrubber and cloth to two sets of clubs. A man and his wife pulled up in a golf cart, stepped out and walked away without so much as a glance.

"You see that?" said Wade. "Not even a thank-you. And look at that cart. It's a mess."

I undid the Velcro strap and lifted the clubs off the back of the cart.

"You know what kind of people don't tip or even look you in the eye?"

"No," I said, even though I'd heard his rant a thousand times.

"Doctors. Cheapest northerners ever." Wade took the clubs from me and hauled them into the shed.

I heard the zip of a pocket opening. Something told me he was planning to get his tip one way or another.

Hot burgers were burning a hole in my passenger seat. I pulled into a BMW dealership and parked between two sparkling 7 Series that brought out the scrapes and dings in my old silver Mustang. Inside, the receptionist greeted me, buzzed my dad and told me to go to his office. His desk was always a mess, and there was an old picture of me from fifth grade that badly needed updating.

"Big game tonight!" said my dad as he strolled into the office.

I held up the bag of burgers. "Brought dinner."

"Sorry, I'm in the middle of closing a deal."

"Don't worry. I'll leave yours here. When's the last time you took a day off?"

"I can sleep when I'm dead."

"You know I hate it when you say that." Long after my mom bailed on my dad, he was still having trouble coping. He always looked kind of worn out. I didn't know if he'd ever get over his wife falling in love with another man. My mom moved to Sarasota and then Atlanta. The farther north she went, the less I spoke to her.

"Thanks for dropping by. Gotta get back and close it."

"Good luck." On my way out, I passed his boss's office and spotted the giant gong that the salespeople hit when they landed a deal. I knew from my dad that business in South Florida was bad all around. Cars baked on lots while malls closed and homes foreclosed.

I turned at the South Coast High sign and parked next to Wade's white Jeep. As I walked behind the school, I heard a voice coming from the basketball court.

"This shouldn't be this difficult."

Through the fence, I spotted Wade and Darren standing in front of Carson and the other two freshmen, Tom and Adrian. All three were in uniform with their heads down. I came onto the court, and Wade tossed my blue math workbook at me. It fell short, its pages splaying open.

"Not only can they not play baseball, but they suck at math."

I picked up the workbook and scanned my homework while Wade continued to fire insults at them the way an Uzi spits out bullets. "I can see where they went wrong," I said. "PEMDAS. You need to multiply what's in the parentheses before—"

"Shut up, Griffin," Wade snapped. "These boys are stupid dogs. And when they don't do what their owner tells them, they must pay. How else are they going to learn?"

Darren shrugged his shoulders as though Wade was waiting for an answer.

I tried to step in again to help the boys. "It goes parentheses, exponents, multiplication—" This only seemed to make Wade angrier.

Wade signaled to Darren, who pulled out an open can of dog food and a plastic spoon. He looked away, offended by the smell, and held it out.

"Your new name, Tom, is Rover. So eat up, Rover," Wade ordered.

Tom dug the spoon into the dog food. After more prodding from Wade, he slowly forced it into his mouth. He gagged, spitting small chunks onto the ground.

Wade and Darren burst into laughter before passing it to Carson.

"Hey," I called out. "It's game time."

Wade looked at Carson. "Your turn, Sparky."

Carson looked at me, his face a complete blank. He took the spoonful and downed it like it was meatloaf.

"That's how you do it," Wade commented. "Good boy, Sparky."

Wade dug the spoon to scoop up more dog food. "Last to go is Buster."

These dog names are so stupid.

I watched Adrian take the dog food. He chewed, looked up at Wade and said, "Seconds, please?"

He was looking for a reaction, but I know Wade, and he doesn't like a suck-up. The boys were dismissed. I warned Wade not to do anything that might come back and bite him.

"Four more months of high school, Griff. You need to relax and enjoy the ride."

I nodded and looked away.

"Is this because of your cousin?" He started laughing before I could answer. "Sparky seemed to enjoy it!"

I followed Wade off the court and toward the baseball field. He howled like a rabid dog the entire way.

Chapter Three

Two balls, two strikes and one out lit up the scoreboard in our game against the Stingrays. The score was tied with three innings left to go in the season opener. I sneaked a peek at the crowd and the bleachers were full. The turnout for the first couple of games, the home-run derby and the playoffs was always good. Everything else was spotty. I saw my dad scurrying past people to an opening on the long bench.

There was no way he had made that sale. The paperwork alone takes forever.

The batter for the Stingrays readied himself as my favorite southpaw on the team, Casey, wound up. Standing where the dirt met the outfield grass, I had Darren to my left at second and Carson at third. I also had the perfect view of every pitch. The batter swung and chipped the ball clumsily toward third. Carson seemed surprised. He grabbed the ball, fumbled it out of his glove and whipped it to first base, off target and late. Wade had to step off the base to get it, and the Stingray was safe on first.

Carson looked upset with himself. Wade punched his fist into his glove. "Come on, Sharks, stay sharp."

The next batter stepped to the plate, his shoulders pressed back, ready to swing. The Stingray on first, giddy to score the go-ahead run, took a leadoff. Casey threw two strikes, but on the next pitch, the batter made contact. I could hear the ball slice through the air, soaring high over my head. Turning with it in my crosshairs, I stepped into outfield territory. The ball was caught too close for comfort at the warning track. The first-base runner tagged up and started toward second. I was the relay man, so the throw came to me. I turned sideways so I could see the play action. I snatched the ball just as the Stingray decided he wouldn't make it and turned back to first. He was right. I whipped the ball to Wade, who extended his glove in an attempt to beat the runner.

Dust shot up in the air. The umpire called, "Safe!"

Wade immediately started to protest the call. "What are you talking about? He's out!"

As shortstop, I also had the responsibility of being captain of the infield. Wade's hands were flailing in the air, and he was a second away from yelling profanities. I stepped in between him and the umpire. "We need you in the game."

He took a deep breath, and I thought he might reach out and slug the ump. Instead, he wisely stepped away.

The Stingray was smirking at Wade, but I had another fire to put out. I stood on the mound with Casey and our catcher, Rafael. I covered my mouth with my glove and told him that the batter got lucky.

"I let it ride too high in the box," Casey said.

"This next one's weak down low, right? I asked.

Casey nodded.

"Go with your slider," Rafael said.

Back at my post, I watched Casey release the slider. There was a noticeable downward yank on the ball as it sharply broke left to right, somewhere between a curve ball and a fastball. Out of the corner of my eye, I saw the guy at first start to run.

"He's going!" Wade shouted.

The moment the batter swung and missed, I launched left. "Got it!" I yelled to Darren as I took second base. Darren covered me in case I screwed up. Rafael fired the ball to second base. The Stingray launched himself at me, determined to steal. All I could do was keep my eyes on the ball. The moment the ball landed in my glove, I dropped it down and smacked it against the sliding Stingray.

The ump took forever to make the call. "Out!"

I smacked gloves with Darren before sending the ball around the horn, first to Wade, who relayed it to Darren, and then off to Carson at third, who tossed it to Casey, completing the circuit. Throwing the ball around after outs was a great way to keep us infielders involved and our arms warmed up. Casey, in a great groove, delivered the last out without a hiccup, and I jogged to the bench.

Carson was quick to find me after the inning.

"I screwed up out there."

"No one scored. So don't sweat it."

"Griff, I'm lucky to be playing infield with you guys." He nudged me with his elbow to follow him. We headed to the far side of the dugout, next to a wooden utility closet. "Adrian and Travis haven't even taken the field yet. They're salivating and know that their opportunity comes from someone like me screwing up."

"The reason you're playing is because you're a natural. The coach sees that." I checked over my shoulder for Wade. He was at the Gatorade cooler. "Carson, you worried about him?"

His eyes traced Wade for a moment. "The guy's a creep. He's got a screw loose, but I can handle him."

"A lot of baseball's about waiting, so it's hard to keep focused a hundred percent of the time."

Carson nodded hesitantly, like I was just giving him an excuse.

"You're not the only one. When we were tanking last season, Coach brought in a guy who said he talks to major leaguers about staying in the game."

"What did he say?"

"He talked about not focusing on winning. Paying attention to the moment. One batter, one pitch at a time. When we get a guy out and the next batter's coming, take a second to drift—check out the crowd or something—then pull yourself back in."

"That actually makes sense."

"You know Wade's crap is just a head game, right?"

Carson nodded.

Brigman's voice rang out. "Hey, Griff, you're on deck!"

I grabbed my black-and-yellow Easton and headed out. I took a couple of practice swings with my $260 bat. It was the most expensive thing I'd bought since my car. I figured they were both worth it because they'd help me get to college.

Rafael went down swinging, and I stepped to the plate, digging my cleats into the dirt. Letting the first pitch slide was kind of a rule of mine. I swung and missed on the second pitch. Not being much of a home-run hitter, I decided there was only one move to make. The pitcher, thinking I was trigger happy, threw an off-speed ball wide of the plate. I jumped on it, stuck my bat out and bunted the ball into the ground. I sprinted to first, beating the ball.

Up next, Wade flexed his muscles on the first pitch and sent it high and far over the fence. Another one for the gators in the pond, I thought as I rounded second base. What college wouldn't give this guy a baseball scholarship? He was a natural-born slugger. Stepping onto home plate, I double-high-fived Wade and turned when I heard a disgusting sound. Adrian hurled, and the smell of dog food cleared the dugout. It took a ten-minute delay and a half can of air freshener, but we hung on to win the opener.

Chapter Four

As I was walking through the courtyard between classes the next day, Carson appeared from behind a curved palm tree.

"Wade around?" he asked, eyes on the ground.

"What, you're not going to ask for permission first?" I said with a big smile. He didn't react. "Carson, you can look at me."

"He's gotta be somewhere." He scanned the crowd and came up empty. "You don't understand. Start walking."

I did and he kept pace directly behind me. "This is ridiculous."

"With Wade in charge, I can't do this."

I stopped and Carson bumped into me.

"Stop screwing around!"

"I'm sorry." I continued forward. "It's just that it looks like I'm talking to myself."

"Not only am I done playing Sparky, but I refuse to be a piece of toilet paper on this guy's shoe."

I turned to look at him, but he wouldn't meet my gaze.

"I signed up to play baseball. That's it."

"I'm confused, Carson. I thought you were okay with all this stupid power-tripping."

"Never mind." He turned and headed in the opposite direction.

It took me a couple of tries to stop him.

"Are you and Wade fighting or something?" he said.

"No, why?"

"At lunch, after you went to your science club, he forced me to sit on the floor while he fed me table scraps."

"Just you? Why?"

"I don't know!" Carson's face turned redder than his hair. "Maybe you should talk to him."

"I'm happy to, but you know Wade. He doesn't even listen to his friends. I could make it worse."

"How could it get any worse, coz?"

By the time I got to work, the last thing I wanted to do was confront Wade. But Carson playing the family card left me no choice. Luckily for me, the change room was empty. Other than getting through my shift, all I wanted to do was collect my As and play ball, both of which I was busting my butt to do. And even still, I needed a scholarship. My worst nightmare was getting into U of Miami and not having the money to pay for it.

Wade was as serious about playing ball as I was, maybe more so. He was gunning for a sports scholarship, and he had done research, staying on top of every magazine, blog and scout Twitter account. He was great for the team, but that didn't excuse him from picking on Carson.

I heard the employee change-room door swing open and drew in a breath. It was only Adrian. He saw me and dropped his eyes to the floor. "Permission to speak, sir," he said.

I was shocked that Wade's wrath was powerful enough to extend outside school. It's not like he was in the room. "Permission granted. What's up?"

"Your homework." He held out my blue-spiraled workbook, avoiding eye contact.

"Thank you, Adrian—uh, Buster."

He seemed nervous, his hands fidgeting.

"What's wrong?"

Adrian's eyes never left the floor.

"What?" I asked angrily. "I'm late for work."

"Permission, sir."

"Yes, you've got permission to talk and look at me."

"Thank you, sir."

He looked awful, dark circles around his eyes. "Grade-twelve math is really hard. I tried my best..."

I flipped open my notebook and riffled through the pages to the previous night's homework. A quick scan showed a number of errors.

"Pythagorean identity is very confusing."

"You could have derived the trigonometric identities using an algebraic equation," I said.

He looked at me, still confused.

"Look, you're not supposed to get this stuff being in grade nine. Let's go. We're late for work." Adrian followed behind me like a dog, and I didn't have the energy to correct him.

At the shed, without saying hello, Wade ordered Adrian to cover for him and then took off. The first cart came in and a couple stepped out. I told Adrian to start on it while I took care of the clubs. Covers for the woods were mismatched and the irons were out of order, but I still smiled and small-talked with the couple, fishing for a tip. Nothing. I dumped their clubs in front of the shed for Adrian. Then I drove the cart behind the shed,

NASCAR-style, and plugged it in to charge.

I raced back just as an old guy in checkered pants and a sweater vest drove up with his wife. I asked them about their game while signaling Adrian to join me behind the cart. "That's the chairman of the Greens Committee," I whispered. Luckily, I recognized him from a picture hanging in the main office. "Guys like him are looking for perfection, and they love pointing out mistakes. Any violation, from a wrinkled golf shirt to an untied shoelace, you'd get a white ticket."

Adrian nodded.

"Now let me show you how to work a tip." I turned to the chairman and his wife as they got out of the cart. "Let me guess. You reached the ninth green, with that slippery slope to the water, using only your driver. Am I right?"

The chairman smiled, reached into his wallet and hesitated on a one-dollar bill before pulling out a fiver.

I thanked him and turned to Adrian. "And that's how you do it."

"That was amazing."

"Well, the way you need—"

The sound of Wade arguing loudly with a man in the parking lot caught our attention. The man had thinning blond hair tied in a small ponytail, and he sported some serious muscles under his golf shirt.

"They're really going at it," Adrian said. "Should we help him?"

Before I could respond, they parted. The man stepped into the clubhouse and Wade started walking our way. I told Adrian to head into the shed.

"You all right?" I asked Wade.

"Not really. And no, I don't want to talk about it."

Two carts skidded to a stop and we each took one. Wade barely touched the clubs.

"Fighting with guests is a new low for you."

He turned to me, looking angry.

"I'm just saying. You know that guy?"

"Yeah...that's Uncle Jim."

33

"Your uncle's a member?"

Wade nodded.

"You guys work out together or something?" I asked, half-serious.

"He owns a fitness club and gives me a membership deal," Wade said.

We took the carts back for charging. "Listen, any chance you can lay off Carson for a while?" I said.

"Did he ask you to say that?"

"No. But I am."

"He's being treated just like the others."

I wasn't going to beg. "Forget it then."

"The problem with Carson is, he thinks he's a better player than he is."

I nodded. *Whatever.*

"And there's only room for one superstar on the Sharks!" Wade walked off.

"Hey," I called out to him.

"What is it, Griff?"

"Nothing." Now wasn't the time to tell him his shirt was untucked.

Chapter Five

Coach Brigman, McKay and Santos entered the locker room just as our team was getting into uniform.

"Can I have your attention?" Brigman said. "I have some bad news."

Everyone stopped and turned. This can't be good, I thought.

Coach cleared his throat. "Our junior player, Carson Miller, was just suspended for the mandatory thirty days."

The locker room buzzed with questions. All I could do was look down at my cell phone in shock. I sent Carson a couple of texts, but he didn't respond. I fired off another one, like a flare gun.

Coach continued. "Unfortunately, it seems as though steroids were found in his locker."

"What?" I shouted. "That's impossible!"

"It was reported to us by the principal."

"Who found the drugs?"

"That's all the information I have for you now. Let me just finish by saying that you all need to stay away from steroids. It might seem like every other major leaguer's on them, but you won't see any of them get into the Hall of Fame. Anabolic steroids are illegal. They cause liver disease, hair loss, high blood pressure, heart attacks...the list goes on."

That just wasn't Carson. He couldn't have gotten into steroids without my knowing. Could he?

"And if that's not enough for you tough guys, they also shrink your privates and make you grow breasts."

Everyone cringed.

"We also found dog food on the basketball courts. Guys, I've been around the block. Just a reminder that we have zero tolerance for hazing. It is a crime, and if caught, you will be suspended." He turned to the younger players. "You two being hazed?"

Adrian and Tom looked at each other, then at the coach. "No," they both said.

As Coach Brigman did his best to turn the team's spirits around, something in me snapped. I broke out of my state of shock and bolted from the locker room. I wasn't going to take this lying down. As I passed the baseball field, I tried opening the gate leading to the school courtyard. It was locked. Of course—school was over a half hour ago.

I started the long run through the side parking lot, making my way around the west perimeter of the school. I deflected stares as I raced by my teammates in uniform. It didn't help that my plastic cleats were grinding on the pavement and sounded like fingernails on a chalkboard. With every step,

I was wearing them down. I came through the front doors and saw Carson in the principal's office with his parents.

I was sweating and panting. The secretary looked at me and asked if I was okay.

Before I could respond, the principal led the Millers out of his office.

"You okay?" I asked Carson as he passed by me. He kept his head down and didn't say a word.

I was on first base with a walk, and the Tigers were leading 2-1. My mind was completely focused on Carson. The worst thing I'd ever seen him do was cheat on a math test. Even then, he'd confessed and demanded a lunch detention. I knew he was innocent. He had to be. People on steroids looked like bodybuilders, not string beans.

The crack of the bat jolted me back into the game. Darren's single into shallow right field forced me to get to second base before the ball. In full sprint, I heard the second baseman shout for it as I transitioned into my go-for-broke dive. I pushed myself forward to beat the ball, coming in with arms stretched out. I hit the ground sliding and sent a cloud of dust into the air. My right hand found the base and I held on to it with everything I had.

"Safe!"

The second baseman argued the call to no effect. I took a time-out to dust myself off and adjust my helmet. My foot safely on second, I gave a thumbs-up to Darren. Carson's replacement, Tom, took some swings and dug himself a hole. He was down two in the count. On the next pitch, he got some aluminum on it, and the ball popped into the air. He was forced to run with two outs, and a Tiger caught it. I stopped in my tracks, annoyed that my diving play was for nothing. *Thanks, Tom.*

Darren grabbed my glove off the bench and tossed it to me. "Carson *was* pretty skinny."

"Huh?"

"So it makes sense that he'd want to bulk up."

"He loved baseball too much to risk screwing it up."

"Maybe he took them because he loved the sport," said Darren. "Just saying."

Casey was having a hard time striking out Tigers. He was down in the count, so he let a ball hang and they homered it. The next batter made contact and drove the ball in my direction. It hit the dirt and jumped out at me. I gloved the ball, and when I reached for it with my throwing hand, I fumbled and dropped it. I scooped it up with plenty of time to still catch the runner. When I released the ball, I gave it some extra whip, but still, somehow, it arrived late.

Tigers were on first and second now. I slammed my fist into my glove, angry that I was off my game. I got back into position and kicked some dirt into the air with my dulled cleats.

"Come on, guys!" Wade called out. "Let's double-play this!"

Psyching myself out over what had happened to Carson was getting me nowhere. To get my head back into the game, I focused on something my dad had said. *Slow the game down. Look at it one pitch at a time.* Casey wound up and released, and the batter made contact, directing the whirling ball toward third base. I ran past second to cover for Darren in case the throw was off. When I looked up, I saw Tom fumbling the ball. Hopes of getting a double play and ending this horrible inning quickly vanished.

"Get to your bag!" I screamed.

Tom looked up at me as the bases loaded.

I walked over to him, my frustration building with every stride. "Hey, Buster."

"Adrian's Buster. I'm Rover."

"Like it matters. That was the perfect double-play setup. Touch the bag and throw to first or second."

"I'm sorry. It was coming in fast."

The Tiger on third base smirked, enjoying the fireworks. We fell behind another three runs before the inning died.

Back on the bench, I couldn't sit still. I downed my water and mumbled to myself until Wade approached.

His eyebrows were furrowed. "Hey, I know that whole Carson thing was hard for you to hear. It's going to be okay."

"Thanks," I said. But I didn't mean it.

"Unfortunately, Carson's actions make us all look bad."

I couldn't believe he'd say that to me, after all the crap he had pulled. "It seemed kind of personal the way you were going after Carson."

Wade took a step back. "Hey, if you think I had anything to do with Carson's suspension, you're wrong. I didn't do anything. Talk to Darren. Talk to anyone."

I stared him down. I was not going to just let this go.

"Come on. We're buds, man."

Yeah, right. He might've considered us buds, but I could still feel it in my gut—Wade was responsible for taking Carson down. And I had to do something about it.

Chapter Six

It was Friday by the time Carson finally showed up at school. He came late, probably hoping he could slip into math unnoticed. When the bell rang to end the period, I practically jumped on him. I fired a thousand questions at him at once.

"What do you want me to say?" He started to walk off.

"Hold up," I said. "I understand that you're upset and dealing with a lot right now, but I'm your friend and your cousin.

You could've answered my phone calls or returned a text."

"I'm on strict curfew at home. They basically took away all my phone privileges. I had to write an apology letter to Coach Brigman, and the school is even forcing me to attend some group-therapy program. But you know what the worst part is?"

"What? Not getting to play baseball?"

"Well, that too. The worst part is Wade's getting away with it."

"He framed you?"

"Don't act surprised."

"I mean, do you have proof that he framed you?"

Carson shook his head.

"So what next?"

Carson shrugged. "Want the best of news of all?"

"Sure."

"Those thirty days of suspension are school days, not including weekends."

"What? That's crazy!"

"Yeah. So I'm out for six weeks! I can't wait that long. I have to find a way to prove that I'm innocent—"

I looked up as Carson suddenly stopped talking.

Wade rounded the corner with Darren. "How you doing, Sparky?"

"Like you care."

"Seriously, we've missed you," Wade said. "You're a much better third baseman than Rover."

Carson gave a half nod.

For a moment, I actually thought Wade might be genuine. Then he ruffled Carson's hair with one hand and snatched his book with the other. "I didn't know dogs could read."

Darren howled.

Wade held the book up, examining it. "*Twenty Thousand Leagues Under the Sea* by Jules Verne."

Carson tried to grab the book, but Wade held it just out of reach. When that bit ran dry, he opened the book and ripped a handful of pages out before throwing it at Carson.

"You didn't have to do that," I said.

"Get your mutt under control," Wade said. He and Darren walked away, still laughing.

Carson's eyes were glued on me. "And I'm not even on the team anymore."

Before I could say anything, he took off into a crowd of students.

Friday-night games always drew the biggest crowd. Attempting to protect my .375 batting average, I stepped to the plate determined to smack the skin off the ball. The Warriors pitcher received a signal from his catcher behind me.

"Go get 'em," Wade called out from the on-deck circle.

My feet and shoulders were square to the pitcher, and my knuckles lined up. The ball came at me and I twisted, shifting my weight forward and pushing my hands out front. The ball dropped and I adjusted my bat, swinging through and making contact. I dropped the bat and sped to first base, beating out the throw. A spatter of applause followed me.

On first, I took a leadoff and watched Wade enter the batter's box. He fired off a couple of intimidating practice swings before sending the first ball into the wire covering behind him. Wade made solid contact on the second pitch, and I watched it soar over the yellow bar outlining the outfield wall. I lost the ball in a sea of palm trees and jogged past second base. At home plate, I turned to the sound of Wade calling out, "Lake Wade!"

As Wade rounded third, in full show-off mode, the guys in the dugout called out, "Ten!" again and again. *Ten homers already?*

Wade bear-hugged me at home plate, dragging me into his celebration. "Ten years from now, they're going to name this field after me."

It was hard to breathe in Wade's tight grip. As I struggled to pull myself away,

I couldn't help wondering at his strength. If Wade had had the steroids to plant on Carson, was it possible he was using them?

As I walked toward my car after the game, I saw Wade and some of the team gathered like they were waiting for me.

"Red Sox are playing in an hour," Wade said. "So hurry up—we're going."

"What?"

"There's no school tomorrow, so relax. It's spring training. You know, the Grapefruit League."

Spend even more time with Wade? No thanks.

"You have to come."

"Why?"

"Because you're driving."

I looked at Darren, Tom, Adrian and Casey.

"Come on, the other guys are already on their way."

After Wade convinced me that his hunk of junk couldn't take five guys, everyone squished into my Mustang. I pulled out of the parking lot and caught up with I-75 north to Fort Myers.

As we cruised down the middle lane, Wade found a song on the radio that he liked enough to belt out as loudly as he could. The words were wrong, the tune was off, and I was the only one who seemed to mind. When an old guy in a Mercedes merged in front of me, Wade hammered my horn until the poor guy moved over.

"Watch this," Wade announced to the guys as he gave the old guy the finger.

A plane appeared below the perfectly white clouds. I sighed because it meant we were almost there. I took the exit for Southwest Florida International Airport, and the JetBlue Park came into focus. When we got inside, I slid into my fifteen-dollar seat on the upper deck of the Green Monster, glad to see the rest of the Sharks.

Casey leaned toward me. "If you ignore the palm trees, it kind of feels like we're in Boston!"

"Also have to ignore the senior citizens," I added.

Casey laughed. "Never seen so many oxygen tanks in one place!"

Wade stood and screamed at the Boston Red Sox, who were being whipped by the Toronto Blue Jays. "Let's go, Red Sox!" He was the loudest person in the cheap seats, smacking his fist into his glove, hungry for a ball. It was like he owned stock in the team.

Boston hit the field in the bottom of the sixth. I got up to get a drink and escape the heat.

"Where you going?" Wade asked from four seats over.

"Refill," I said, shaking my drink.

"Let one of the mutts do it."

"It's okay—I need some shade for a minute."

"Tom," he said, "take care of this."

Tom popped up out of his seat on command, but I stopped him. "It's okay, Tom. Enjoy the game."

Wade glared at me. "What's your problem? He's honored to do it for you."

Someone behind me yelled for me to sit down. I felt Darren grab my arm and yank me into my seat.

"Hey, Tom, while you're up"—Wade pointed to an ad on the side of the old-school scoreboard—"grab us some Buds."

Adrian got up to help and Wade told him to hurry back, reminding him that he was on standby to chase down any home-run balls.

I slunk back into my seat. Rafael turned to me. "Talk about a dream job. Hundred and sixty-two games, different city every week, private jet, hotels."

"Playing baseball every day. No job at the golf club."

"The fans...the groupies."

"Heard they have an amazing pension and health benefits."

Rafael shot me a look.

"I mean, the groupies."

Rafael smiled and pointed to a Red Sox left fielder. "The only things between him and us are some college scouts, one to four years of a degree, more scouts and a major-league draft."

51

I nodded. "'Cause we already got the talent."

Our quick high five was interrupted by Tom and Adrian. They each balanced a full tray of soft drinks.

"Where's my beer?" Wade asked.

"Got carded," Tom said sheepishly.

"You guys suck."

The boys handed the drinks out to everyone. "How much?" I asked when they passed me one. Tom shook his head before holding out a spring-training Red Sox baseball hat.

"For shade." He tossed it at me with the tag still on it.

The crack of a bat and the sound of cheering close by caught my attention. I spotted a fly ball making a run for the Green Monster. I stood with the rest of my section. When I realized it was sinking fast, I jumped out of my seat and stood at the edge of the wall, my new baseball hat stretched out. The baseball came in like a meteor, smacked into my hat and forced it from my grip. I watched my hat drop onto the outfield with the ball, Wade laughing the whole time.

Chapter Seven

As I drove toward I-75 after the game, my ego bruised, I tried to ignore Wade's taunting. "The one that got away," he kept saying, trying to get a rise out of me.

We were nearing the freeway when Wade shouted, "Turn here."

"Why?"

"I gotta go."

I turned right, passing a strip mall and a Wells Fargo bank before I found a secluded spot. "This okay?"

"Little farther."

Manicured lawns and perfectly placed trees appeared on the right. That was usually the first sign that a golf club was ahead.

"Okay, U-turn it here and pull over."

I put the car in Park, and Wade ran out. I took the opportunity to apologize to the three guys clumped in the backseat.

Wade's voice rang out, "Guys, you gotta see this."

I adjusted my sunglasses, a bit frustrated. "What now?"

Wade came back to the car and pointed to Adrian and Tom. "Get out, now."

Darren followed, and after a long minute I killed the engine and slammed my door shut.

"Check her out," Wade said.

I took a few steps onto a patch of uncut grass and saw a small lake surrounded by trees. The hum of the freeway could be heard in the distance. "What are you looking at?"

"That." Wade pointed.

I took a quick step back when I spotted an alligator. Its thick tail was on the edge of the water.

"She looks hungry."

"Whatever you say, Wade. Okay, everyone back in the car."

"Hold on," Wade said, examining it from afar. "You know, these creatures won't attack unless we do."

"He's right," Darren added.

Wade turned to Tom and Adrian. "You two want to get out of hazing for the rest of the year?" He didn't wait for them to respond. "All you have to do is touch it."

Darren was amused, clapping his hands together in anticipation.

"You don't have to do this," I said to the boys firmly.

Tom looked at me and then Wade. "Together or separately?"

"Don't matter." Wade looked at me. "I'm disappointed, Griff. Well, at least it's clear who's in charge."

Tom stepped toward the alligator, with Adrian close behind.

"I want a proper touch," Wade said loudly, probably hoping to get a reaction from the gator.

Standing there, I felt just as responsible for what might go wrong as Wade. I'm the one with the keys, I told myself. I could head out whenever I wanted.

The two boys were only three strides away. Wade and Darren were silently laughing.

I stepped toward Wade and muttered, "Call this stupid thing off."

"Why, Griff? I'm enjoying the show. Question is, why aren't you?"

I didn't respond.

Tom's and Adrian's hands were now outstretched toward the resting gator, but my focus wasn't on them. It was on the gator. Its large green eyes divided by black slits were watching back. Sharp white teeth jutted out of its elongated mouth. "You don't have to do this," I said to the boys.

A few inches from the gator, nerves got the best of Tom. As he flinched, the gator snapped the air. The boys recoiled to a safe distance, and I started to breathe again.

"You failed," Wade announced. "This animal sensed your fear and you lost."

"It's a three-hundred-pound beast," Adrian pleaded, tears welling up in his eyes. "So give us a break!"

"Nothing more than pathetic excuses—"

"Let's just go," I said, cutting Wade off.

"No. I know what these two are thinking." Wade paused. "They think that I don't have the guts to do it myself."

"Yes, you do. Happy?" I took my keys out and shook them. "Let's roll."

Wade looked at me, his fists clenched and his jaw locked in place. Just when I thought he was going to come at me, he turned and stepped toward the gator. He crouched over it like he was taking a bow. He tapped its nose with his hand, and the gator's mouth popped open, exposing its teeth.

Tom and Adrian looked at me and I shrugged, nervously playing with my keys.

"Put them away," Wade said, throwing me a quick look. "Darren," Wade said, staring down the gator, "get out your phone and record this."

The gator closed its mouth and Wade tapped it again, reopening it. The boys applauded, but he wasn't done. He used his other hand to press up on its chin, raising its head.

While Wade was distracted, I took the opportunity to reimburse Tom for the hat he had bought me. I slid a twenty from my back pocket over to him. Again, he refused to take the money.

Wade cupped the alligator's chin and forced it even higher. The gator struggled to get free but couldn't.

I knew how hard it was to save twenty bucks and felt bad that Wade had forced Tom to spend his money. As I rolled up the twenty-dollar bill, I watched Wade force the alligator back onto its hind legs. It was hard to tell which one was the animal. He turned to make sure we were all watching him show off just as I leaned over to tuck the money in Tom's back pocket.

"What are you doing?"

I didn't respond to Wade. The alligator wriggled free, and Wade stepped back as it snapped at him, barely missing his arm. The gator, also fed up with Wade, turned and slunk back into the water.

"Nicely done," Adrian said, sucking up.

Wade pushed past him toward me. "You're a senior. Start treating him like the dog he is."

"No, I'm sorry," Tom said. "It was my fault."

Wade ignored him and stepped closer to me. I could see my reflection in his sunglasses. "What is your problem?"

I stood my ground. "I'm tired of these games."

"I'm saying this because we're friends. You pull this again, with me or my two mutts, and I'm gonna take you down."

He didn't move and neither did I.

"Understand me?"

I felt myself tense up, and I had to decide quickly whether I was going to fight or back down. Out here on the side of the road, with no clue if anyone was on my side, the decision was crystal clear.

Chapter Eight

Monday morning, I stood in the school parking lot as Carson rode up on his bike. He pulled off his helmet. "Why am I meeting you at school at 8:00 AM?"

"Wade is a conniving liar."

"Tell me something I don't know."

"I'm pretty sure he's using the same stuff that he planted in your locker."

"So you aren't friends anymore? What happened?"

"Long story."

61

Carson nodded. "Look, I'm sorry for being on edge lately. Baseball's my life. I'm going crazy having nothing to do after school."

"I get it. Wade really crossed the line with me. Besides, I've been thinking. Blood is thicker than water."

"So, does that mean you're gonna help get me back on the team?"

I flicked my fingers. "Follow me." The doors to the school were locked, so I hit the intercom button. It took two minutes for a caretaker to show up. I told him we were there for a debate-team meeting and were locked out.

He seemed skeptical at first but finally let us in after getting us to write our names down. We headed for Wade's locker.

"You put down my real name?"

"No, of course not." I took a long look at Wade's locker. "I'm hoping Wade keeps his steroids in here." I pulled on the door to see if it would somehow magically open. It didn't. I pulled a piece of aluminum out of my pocket. It was shaped like a rectangle with a small triangle on top. "I found this trick on YouTube last night. It's like a shim, made from a Coke can."

Carson laughed. "Who *are* you?"

"Just watch this." I placed the triangle inside the top left side of the lock and wedged it in. Then I wrapped the shim's rectangle arms around the loop of the lock. "Here we go." I pulled the loop upward while pushing the handmade shim down at the same time.

The lock popped open, and I jumped in surprise.

"Nice one!" Carson said, patting me on my back.

"Ready?"

"Yes."

I pulled the door open and had to take a step back. Textbooks were crammed on top of molding food. Old gym shorts and a dozen empty water bottles filled the small locker. On the bottom were all of his Lake Wade baseballs. They were so deteriorated that the leather was peeling off most of them. I started breathing only through my mouth as I sifted through the locker.

"Anything?" Carson asked, looking over my shoulder.

"Nothing. Wish I had brought rubber gloves." Thinking he might have a hiding spot, I pulled on the shelf, tapped on the back and even tried to lift the bottom metal base. Nothing. I stepped back from the locker's stench, happy to start breathing normally again. "I really think he's using."

"How else could he get stuff to plant on me?"

"Plus all those home runs." I closed the door and slid the lock back on. "I don't know where he's keeping his stash. But even if we can't find the drugs, that doesn't mean we can't find his dealer."

"I like the way you think," Carson said.

"Maybe that'll lead to proof that he's using."

"But if he finds out what you're doing, he's going to kill you."

"Don't care."

Carson smirked. "Let's go get a coffee. I want to hear this long story."

Never having been in the market for steroids or any other drug before, it was a rough beginning. We started with the yearbook, picking out people we thought might be users. All we really had to go on were stereotypes drawn from years of watching television. But we kept striking out. How hard could it be to find drugs at a high school?

After a few days, we still had nothing, so we took a chance on another stereotype. Lewis Reynolds, who always wore flip-flops and sported a permanent tan, was big into surfing. Based on a B movie I had seen recently, I figured there was no way he wasn't smoking up after a totally radical ride or during a beach bonfire party.

Carson and I followed Lewis to a restaurant called Snorkels. I found parking and spotted Lewis already in line, waiting to order food. Snorkels was painted bright green and orange. Wetsuits, flippers and other diving equipment were attached to the wall. Everything on the menu was ten dollars or less. In line, I kept my distance from Lewis.

"What should we do?"

"Order."

We took our fried-fish sandwiches and French fries outside to an empty picnic table. I sat facing Lewis while Carson provided a barrier between us. Lewis met up with two friends and worked on his food with one hand while he texted with the other.

"I don't know how to do this, Carson."

"Just go up to them and say, 'I'm looking to score drugs.'"

"Sure. Why don't you go for it?" I took a big bite out of my sandwich. It was too hot.

"This was your idea."

"But I'm the one helping you!"

"Yeah," Carson said, "and you get nothing from Wade being kicked off the team."

"Fine," I said, stretching my neck, trying to shake off the nerves. I held out my hand, and Carson placed the fifty dollars we had both coughed up into it. Going to start small talk with Lewis was worse than asking a girl out. Not knowing what to say when I got to his table, I dropped to one knee and pretended to tie a shoelace. Too bad I was wearing my Converse slip-ons.

I looked up and pretended I knew him. "Hey, Lewis, right?"

He looked at me, trying to place my face.

"How's it going?"

His friends didn't look up from their phones. Too busy checking the surf report, I guessed.

"Ah, not bad."

"How's the surf season so far?" I asked, wondering if surfers even had seasons. *Enough stalling—just ask.* "Look, can you hook me up?" I said under my breath.

Lewis turned to his friends. Apparently, I had piqued their interest. "So, because I surf, you assume I smoke pot or something?"

I took a step back. "I'm sorry."

He broke out into laughter. "Have a seat, bra."

I did.

"So you go to SCH?"

"Yeah."

"Whatcha want?"

"Whatcha have?" I asked, trying to fit in.

"This isn't Target."

His friends laughed until I said, "Steroids."

"Not on my usual menu because it's tricky to get. That stuff comes from labs in China, you know."

I nodded.

"You got cash?"

I put the assortment of bills on the table.

"Whoa." Lewis and his friends stood, stepping away from the table. "Ever heard of the Five-O?"

I was confused. My little deal was quickly falling apart. "Huh?"

"The fuzz, my man. Put the dead presidents away."

I stuffed the cash back into my pocket, and Lewis sat back down. "How much you have?"

"Fifty."

He held out his Styrofoam takeout container and signaled me to put the money in it. One of his friends counted the money under the table. He nodded, confirming what I'd said.

"Won't get you much—barely a starter kit."

"It's all I need."

"You play sports or just trying to Schwarzenegger up?"

"Bulk up," I said, wondering what it mattered to him.

Lewis nodded. "Meet me back here, same time on Monday."

"Thank you."

Lewis gave me a funny look. I wondered if he was thinking I was totally out of my element. And why did I thank him? You don't thank a drug dealer.

He stood, patted my shoulder and left.

I watched him go and then speed-walked to the safety of my car. A few minutes later, Carson arrived.

"So?" he asked.

"Done." I felt confident, like I did after a double play. The plan was officially in motion.

Chapter Nine

The next day at practice, Coach Brigman announced that everyone was working the infield. "Whether you're a pitcher or outfielder, I want you here. Now toss a ball back and forth for warm up."

I partnered with Tom.

"Focus on transferring your weight into the throw," Coach Brigman said. He had McKay and Santos walking around, making sure we were following instructions.

I guess practice is the one place where Wade's rules for the freshmen don't apply, I thought. Hard to throw the ball at someone who's not allowed to look at you. Next, I stepped closer to Tom, and Brigman had us squat down. I caught Tom's bouncing pass in my glove and threw it back at him. The more the drill went on, the more I felt pain building in my thighs and abdomen. "This is worse than when he made us do a hundred sit-ups."

"Yeah, I can't feel my legs," Tom said.

"Problem is"—I snatched the ball and returned it to him—"I can feel mine." Just when I was about to keel over, Coach Brigman stepped forward.

"Down on one knee and same drill. Chest out, but face your partner."

Facing sideways but looking at Tom, I picked the ball out of the grass and flung it back at him. The pain vanished.

"I appreciate you trying to stick up for us with that alligator," Tom said.

"No problem. It was a stupid situation and you guys—"

"Next time," Tom interrupted, "please don't."

"Why?"

"It makes it worse for us."

I nodded. *I was just trying to help.*

After doing the same drill on the other knee, we were told to get down on both knees. "Five balls," Coach said. "Your partner throws while you make the catch with one hand behind your back. If you miss or you fall over, you and your partner can get some water."

The first few rounds back and forth were no problem, but then it got tough to focus. It didn't help that I could see who missed and who fell off position. At the far end, I saw Wade and Casey going strong. Another round and the competition thinned out. Wade and Casey were left, plus Darren and Rafael.

"Hold up," Coach Brigman said, clapping his hands. He got the six of us up and repositioned in a circle, facing each other. "Keep one hand behind your back like before. If your throw's off, you're out."

I caught Wade's eyes on me and looked away. It was strange practicing with him, knowing that I was in the middle of a plan to set him up.

Coach tossed the ball to Wade and said, "Go." Wade whipped it at Tom. His reflexes weren't quick enough, and he was the first eliminated. Casey sent a curve ball at me, and I tracked it before securing it. I eyed Wade, then sent a low, fiery ball to Darren instead. Darren tried to get a glove on it, but missed. He stood and walked past me, gritting his teeth. Casey was next to go.

Wade, Rafael and I were left. Coach passed the ball to Rafael, who must've seen Wade as a threat, because he practically lobbed it to him.

Wade put some extra muscle into his throw, almost blowing me over.

I could play dirty too, I thought. I sent the ball down low into the grass. It took an unpredictable bounce, flying up and into a collision course with Wade's face. He swatted it away, protecting himself, and the ball bounced to the side.

I raised my hands in celebration.

Wade stood. "You call that a throw?"

"Looked like one to me."

Wade approached, and I jumped from my knees to my feet.

Coach Santos stepped in. "Boys, cool off."

"Yeah," Coach Brigman added. "You're both out."

Rafael stood, and I joined in on congratulating him. Losing had never felt so good.

Chapter Ten

In the long shadow of a palm tree, I sat on a bench with Carson outside of Snorkels. Ditching our last class before lunch gave us a chance to do some research. Carson hovered over my phone as I googled anabolic steroids. Wikipedia had too much information, and other sites tried to lure me in with pictures of bodybuilders. "I just want to know what I'm buying."

"Click on the ESPN site," Carson said. "What's your plan once you get these steroids, exactly?"

"Not sure. But there's no way Lewis is going to admit selling drugs to Wade if I seem like a narc." I skimmed over the scientific mumbo jumbo and right to a description of how they're taken. "'Steroids can be taken orally or they can be injected,'" I read.

"I hate needles," Carson said.

"Don't worry, we're not the ones taking them."

"Yeah, but what if Lewis wants to make sure we're legit and forces us to take them?"

"Then we bolt."

Carson nodded. "I'm good with that."

"Here's what the coach was talking about. Side effects are development of breasts, pain while urinating, premature heart attacks—"

"Shrinking of private parts!" Carson shrieked, loud enough to catch the attention of a passerby.

"Look at this. Steroid users have severe mood swings. They range from 'extreme temper to feelings of invincibility to aggressive behavior.'" I looked at Carson. "That describes Wade perfectly. He's got a wicked temper. And invincibility—well, I told you about that stunt with the alligator."

"Aggression too. Look how he treats the freshmen."

"Exactly." I clicked on another site that warned of something called 'roid rage. "If you take large doses, violent behavior can turn to brutal attacks and even murder."

"Maybe we shouldn't be messing with Wade."

"So that's it?" I said. "You want to give up?"

Carson didn't have an answer, so I moved back to my search and clicked on images. The screen filled with grotesque pictures of extreme bodybuilders, dumbbells and close-ups of the drug. I clicked on an image of colored vials filled with liquid steroids. The next picture showed green and white pills.

"Ready?" Carson asked.

"Absolutely not."

I shifted uncomfortably on the bench, barely able to put a dent in my fish burger. I felt a tap on my shoulder and saw one of Lewis's friends. He wore dark reflective sunglasses, and the top of his head stuck out of an army-green visor. The word *Callaway* was written on it in red.

I got up. "You going to finish your fries?" Carson said.

Lewis's friend pointed to Carson and gestured that he should come too.

Carson lagged behind me as I trailed Lewis's friend past some peach stuccoed stores. The sidewalk ended and we hopped over a row of perfectly trimmed shrubs. Lewis stood beside his car, parked near a Dumpster. It was a silver Honda Civic with tinted windows and a large sunroof. I quickly calculated that he was probably making more money than I was and working fewer days. Working smarter, not harder, as my dad would say.

Lewis waited for us to approach. "First, I'm not selling you drugs."

I was confused.

"I'm offering them to you."

"Okay?"

"There's a big difference. I'm just providing a service to sad lowlifes like yourself who can't live without drugs."

I looked at him. Was he joking, or was he trying to protect himself somehow?

"I'm doing you a favor."

I offered a thank-you, but he didn't say, "You're welcome."

"One more thing. Steroids aren't easy to find, so it's going to be an extra fifty."

I knew that I was being ripped off, but I also didn't have much of a choice. There was no one around but us. "Can I speak with my friend first?"

Lewis nodded.

With my back to the boys, I told Carson to empty his pockets. He was about to argue, but I cut him off. "What do you want me to do? They don't negotiate or give refunds."

He held up a ten and I grabbed it. I handed Lewis twenty-one dollars and change. "It's all we have."

Lewis examined it before nodding. One of his friends grabbed the money and held out a candy container. He shook it, and I heard something rattling around inside. I held out my hand, but he placed it on the ground and kicked it to me.

"Nice doing business with you," Lewis said, already moving toward his Civic.

I grabbed the container and hauled Carson back to the storefront. I popped the container lid open. Inside were two white pills.

"Let me see." Carson examined them. "Right shape and color."

I poured them into my cupped hand and rolled them around. "What's that?"

Carson held one up. "Looks like something's been scratched off it."

We could both make out the remnants, in red, of the word *Tylenol* and the number *500*.

He slapped the pill into my hand. "They ripped us off!"

Behind us, I heard a honk and saw Lewis peel out of the parking lot, laughing.

Frustrated but more embarrassed, I kept moving. "Let's go to plan B."

"What's plan B?"

"I don't know yet."

"Think my haddock burger's still over there?" Carson started to move toward the bench.

I shot out my arm, stopping him. Down a narrow walkway to the restrooms, I saw Wade with someone I didn't recognize. Wade was holding a wad of cash and counting it.

We took cover behind a car. "You know the other guy?"

"No," Carson said. "But this plaza is ground zero for drug transactions."

"And I think we just bumped into plan B." We ducked when we saw Wade and the mysterious teen exit. Hunched over, I scurried to my Mustang in time to see them get into their cars. Wade was first to leave, but we decided to find out who the other person was. I kept my distance, staying two car lengths behind. When he pulled into a gas station, I put my flashers on and pulled over.

He pulled out of the station and did a U-turn, and I struggled to keep up with him.

At the next street there was no light, so I was able to make a quick turnaround.

"Where do you think he's going?"

"I don't know. Do drug dealers have a hangout?"

He started to slow down, crossing three lanes before pulling into our high school.

"This just got a lot more interesting," Carson said.

I parked far enough away to keep a low profile. We jumped out of the car, still tailing him. "How do we not know this guy?"

"Don't know," Carson said. "Lewis was a bust, but we can still bring Wade down through his dealer. Won't put me back on the team, but at least getting some justice will be sweet."

"How're we going to do that?" I asked.

"We'll shake him down! Threaten to report him unless he rats on Wade."

"Or we could just report this guy to the principal."

"We have no evidence," Carson said.

"But we have a time and a location. The more details we have, the more the principal and coach will know we're not lying."

We stopped when we saw him go into a classroom. We found out from someone heading in behind him that it was grade-eleven science.

"Ready for the good news?" I asked Carson.

"Yeah."

"Since I did the deal, you get to report all this to the principal."

"He won't believe me. He'll just think I'm trying to get even with Wade. Plus we don't even know this guy's name."

"Just take out your phone and snap a quick picture."

I pushed Carson toward the door of the classroom.

Chapter Eleven

Carson promised me he reported what we saw to the principal. But over a week later, I was still waiting for the tsunami to strike and take down Wade. There was nothing. It was business as usual. I tried to keep my distance from Wade as he continued to treat Tom and Adrian like dogs.

At our next game against the Lions, Coach Brigman came into the locker room looking disappointed. He stared down at his clipboard until everyone else noticed too.

"This isn't how I like to lead into a game. I have someone here who'd like a few minutes of your time." He stepped aside. "Mr. Tom Martino."

Martino came in and put down a large cloth shopping bag. I recognized him but couldn't place him. At least six feet tall, he wore circular horn-rimmed glasses, and his short hair was parted perfectly at a forty-five-degree angle. "I'm the assistant principal of attendance and discipline. Sharks, it saddens me to be here, because I know you're all focused on winning this game. You make the school proud." He looked at each of us, studying our faces. "I've been running an investigation into the use of performance-enhancing steroids on all of our school's teams."

I took a deep breath. *Finally!* If I could have jumped up and cheered, I would have.

"Boys, at this time I'm not accusing any one of you specifically. But you need to know that we have a board policy that states zero tolerance when it comes to drugs, including anabolics. They are illegal, and Florida state schools have made drug testing mandatory. I take full responsibility for letting the testing slip by in the past, but not anymore."

Wade raised his hand and got the nod from Martino. "As captain of this team, it makes me really angry that someone would stoop to taking drugs. We're just trying to play baseball and win games. This is the last thing we need." He slowed his words down, stressing every syllable. "Whoever's doing this should just confess."

I rolled my eyes, hoping they wouldn't buy into his act.

"I appreciate what you're saying," Mr. Martino said. "But that doesn't change what we have to do." He reached into his bag and pulled out a small see-through cup with an orange lid. "I need everyone to fill one of these up."

"Drink up if you need inspiration, boys," Coach Brigman said. Wade pulled a bottle of Gatorade out of his locker. Martino started to read the names on each cup, handing them out. I joined a line leading to the urinals and hoped I'd get into one of the two stalls. At least there was no way for Wade to get out of this. Ahead of me in line, he looked strangely confident.

The line moved slowly. As I reached the door to the small restroom, Wade turned from a urinal to leave. When he walked past me, he winked, and I knew we couldn't have nailed him. I looked around, wondering if he'd switched cups with someone. Then I got a nudge from behind. It was my turn.

Mr. Martino wished us a good game and headed out with a bag filled with urine specimens.

"Get your heads in the game," Coach Brigman said, "and let's go win this one."

Sharks started to follow him out until Wade blocked the exit to the field. "Who called him?"

There was no answer.

"Come on, you bunch of rats. Who's trying to destroy this team?" Again, no answer. "How are we supposed to focus and have a chance of making it to the finals when we have a witch hunt going on?"

He walked past Tom and Adrian, patting them each on the head. "One of my dogs already went down. I guess the question is, who's going to be next?"

I started to worry about him planting steroids again. Was he slipping them into players' water bottles? Did he do it to me? I hadn't felt any side effects, but I guessed even the smallest trace could be detected.

"Come on, guys. Better to come clean now. Maybe the school will show mercy."

I was a little confused. I figured Wade would want to lay low. Becoming the anti-steroid spokesperson made him stand out. I guess the best defense is a good offense.

"If any of you are doing 'roids, then just come out and say it!"

No one stepped forward. Wade spun around and took off to the field.

We were tied 1-1 in the top of the ninth inning in a complete sleeper game. There's nothing like a steroids allegation to bring down team spirits. Still, I didn't regret what

Carson and I had done. I wasn't going to feel bad for trying to take down someone who was cheating, conniving and abusing people to land himself a baseball career.

The Lions called up their heavy hitter.

"Let's get this guy out!" I yelled, trying to wake the team out of its slumber.

The hitter stepped to the plate, crowding it. While he took some practice swings, I took a quick scan of the infield. Darren was in position on second, Tom was standing too close to third base for this hitter, and Wade didn't seem to care. I signaled for Tom to take a few steps toward me.

Casey sent the pitch fast and low, but in the strike zone. The hitter swung behind it, still making contact. The ball traveled low and hit the grass to the right of the pitcher's mound. I leaped forward, not waiting for the ball to come to me. Before it could bounce again, I got my glove on it. Quick with the catch and release, I whipped it to Wade while still moving forward. It was on target but low. I knew he'd accuse me of doing it on purpose.

As he stepped forward, the ball hit the dirt and took an unpredictable bounce, left and up.

It landed in the grass. Not being able to watch, I dipped the brim of my hat to block the action.

I was relieved to hear applause. The runner was out. One more out to go and then we would be up to bat.

The next player stepped to the plate and swung at the first pitch. He made contact and punched the ball over the outfield fence. In an instant, we were down by one run.

We entered the bottom of the ninth and Coach Brigman gave us the quick all-or-nothing talk.

"How bad do you want it?" he asked.

"Bad!" we shouted back.

I sat at the front end of the bench with my batting glove on. I tried my best to ignore Wade as he complained about my throw. Our first at bat, Darren, went down swinging. I grabbed my bat and stood in the on-deck circle. Tom marched to the plate. I took a practice swing and made sure to wind my bat all the way back. I raised my leading foot and then stepped into the imaginary pitch.

Strike one.

I focused on being straight as an arrow, reminding myself not to swing down on the pitch.

Strike two.

I imagined the path of a ball and tried to accelerate as deeply as possible into it.

Strike three.

Chapter Twelve

Tom blew past me with his head slung low. With two outs, the pressure to keep this game alive was on my shoulders. In the batter's box, I dug my cleats into the dirt and stared down the Lions' pitcher. I knew he wasn't in a hurry to throw anything over the plate. I watched the first pitch land outside and low. The second pitch started high, and I made the split-second decision to make the most of it. My bat made contact. It wasn't the kind of hit that would bring the people in the stands to their feet, but I wasn't going for that. The ball arced over the second baseman, and I arrived safely at first. It felt good to have the pressure on someone else until Coach Santos, who was first-base coach, patted me on the shoulder.

"So there are two outs and no one else on base. Rafael's up to bat, and we need to generate a run. Here's what I want you to do..."

The Lion covering first base started to listen, and that's exactly what Coach Santos wanted him to do.

"I want you to make sure the bunt hits the ground before you run."

The Lion heard the word *bunt* and took a step farther infield. I took three steps off the bag. The pitcher reached the top of his throw and I took another quarter step away from first. Crouched down, I waited for the pitcher to start his windup and then took off. I barreled forward with second base in my crosshairs. The ninety-foot sprint seemed to take forever. I got low and extended both my arms, sliding headfirst.

I looked through the settling dirt to see the umpire doing a sweeping motion with his arms. "Safe!"

I stood and called for time. The crowd cheered, the umpire nodded, and I stepped off the base to dust myself off. I got back on base, Rafael stepped to the plate, and I took a small leadoff. He was caught watching the first two pitches roll in as strikes. The third pitch was an obvious ball. Then came a failed attempt to pick me off at second.

"Let's go, Rafael!" I called out.

Next pitch came in low and outside. Rafael stretched for it and made contact. The ball flew over my head and I took off. I was almost at third and running at top speed when Coach McKay threw both hands out to stop me. Believing that I was the tying run and visualizing myself as the team hero, I blew past his double stop signs and around third toward home plate. Then, over my shoulder, I spotted the baseball flying to the catcher.

I hit the brakes halfway between third and home.

Both fielders tried to make the tag on me. With each throw, they got closer. I was under attack and had to make my move. I faked forward to entice the catcher. He finally bit. I backpedaled to third and dropped. The catcher reached out to tag me and I speed-crawled, touching third base with no time to spare.

Coach McKay tried to let me have it, but it was hard to hear him over the applause.

I looked down at myself and could barely make out the white of my uniform.

"Rafael's on second, so only take a small leadoff," Coach McKay said.

I nodded and turned my attention to home plate as Wade stepped up. He watched the first pitch go down the middle for a strike. I wondered if he'd sabotage a possible win just to leave me hanging.

The next pitch came in. Strike. Wade turned to look at me.

I couldn't believe it. After everything it took to get me here, he was going to make sure I didn't make it home.

Third and fourth pitches were balls. With the count two and two, he swung late and dropped his bat on the ground like he was upset with himself.

I left third for the lonely walk to the dugout. I had a perfect view of the stands emptying out.

As I got to the parking lot, I spotted Wade standing next to Darren's car. Wade didn't seem too upset by the loss at all. He and Darren actually looked like they were going out to celebrate. My phone vibrated in my pocket. It was Carson. "What's up?"

"Where have you been?" He sounded agitated.

"Baseball."

"While you've been doing that, guess who showed up at my support group?"

Darren and Wade were laughing and making enough noise to distract me.

"Can I call you back?"

"The drug dealer!"

"Who?"

"Wade's drug dealer."

I lowered my voice. "That doesn't make sense."

"It makes perfect sense. Can you think of a better place to reach buyers?"

I opened the car door. "I'm on my way."

"The session just ended."

"When's the next one?"

"Tuesday after the long weekend."

I endured a Friday baseball practice and a three-day weekend with my dad in Tampa. The whole time, I couldn't stop thinking about confronting the dealer at Carson's next session. When class ended Tuesday, I jumped into my car with Carson and was the first out of the parking lot. He directed me west along Immokalee Road. I parked in front of a two-story building with a sign that said *Business Center*.

"You going to wait here?" Carson asked.

"No, I want to see this guy in action. What's his name?"

"Derek."

The waiting room of the Department of Children and Families—Receiving Facility looked like it belonged in a doctor's office. Past the secretary and into a room, there were about ten teens, all with their heads down, focused on their phones.

Right behind Carson, a silver-haired woman with kind eyes stopped me.

"I don't have anybody new on my list for this afternoon."

"I thought I'd just try—"

"You do realize that this is a drug and alcohol group-therapy session."

"Yes," I said, pausing for a moment. "I do drugs. Well, steroids."

She examined me suspiciously.

"And a little alcohol."

"Are you still in school?"

"Yes." I wasn't sure if she was buying my story.

"I'm not here to judge or criticize you, but I do need a referral from your guidance counselor and a note from your guardian."

I gazed down, trying to look as sad and confused as possible.

"Since you're here, you can watch. My name's Lisa."

"Griffin."

I grabbed a chair and placed it in the circle.

Lisa stood in the center of the group and began her introduction. I let my gaze drift around the room, quickly spotting Wade's dealer, Derek.

"Addicts have secrets, shame and guilt," Lisa continued. "You need to open up and let it out. I promise that you won't be judged here."

I stood with everyone else as they formed a football huddle. Like the others, I repeated Lisa's words. "I am important. I value my life." I looked up and made eye contact with Carson. "I have a bright future. I am loved."

The group huddle broke up and Lisa told everyone to pick a corner of the room based on what color they were feeling right now.

I joined Carson and we followed Derek to the blue corner.

"Tell the people in your color group why you chose it," Lisa continued.

I turned to Carson, keeping my voice low. "I have to say, this guy is brilliant. Everyone here is a possible customer."

"So, what now?"

"We can follow him for two weeks and build evidence or we can just talk to him." Again, Carson was happy to let me take the lead. When Derek's partner moved to someone else, he turned to me.

"So why blue?" he asked.

"I don't know."

"Well, I chose it because it reminds me of the ocean."

I nodded. "So, listen, can you hook me up?"

"What? You're joking, right?"

"Derek, I know you're dealing—"

Carson stepped forward. "Yeah, we saw you with Wade."

He looked at us and smiled. "You two are morons. I'm not the dealer."

"You're not?" I asked.

He shook his head. "Wade is."

Chapter Thirteen

I was shocked.

How long had Wade been dealing?

Lisa asked everyone to stop, and she pointed at me. "Griffin. Please share with the group why you chose your color."

"Uh, I picked blue because of the ocean."

The group looked at me, confused.

"Never mind."

"No, please explain."

"Well, sometimes I feel like I'm underwater, and when I look up I feel the pressure of the world on top of me."

"Very profound," Lisa said.

I was impressed that I was able to spit that out.

"Now, I want everybody to pick a different corner. Your options are"—she pointed as she named the corners—"fall, winter, spring and summer."

I followed Derek to the spring corner. "So how did he pass the drug test?"

He paused. "There's a little rule in this world that I like to follow. Trust no one." He changed corners, and I stayed with him.

"Maybe he switched the labels," I said.

Derek ignored me.

"Or does he have someone on the inside who can help him?"

He looked at Carson. "Tell your friend to leave."

Lisa interrupted. "You guys seem to be deep in discussion. Derek, please share."

"I picked fall because I feel like I'm falling. Like, you know, leaves controlled by the wind."

The group clapped.

"Help me and I'll leave," I whispered to Derek.

He sighed. "It's not that hard to cover up drugs."

"Like how?"

"Maybe he had a clean sample on him."

I thought back to the Gatorade bottle in Wade's locker. His smug smile waiting in line.

"Look, Wade is not the type of person you want to mess with," Derek continued. "I know someone who didn't pay up and Wade put him in the hospital."

The next day after school, Carson and I followed close behind Wade's Jeep. "Keep your phone out and be ready to take pictures and video."

"Gotta admit, I'm a little worried about what Derek said."

"You know, Carson, at some point you need to man up. Otherwise, why are you here?"

Carson nodded, focusing on his phone.

Wade pulled into a small plaza. He parked and walked into Club 21 Fitness. I spotted a burger dive on the corner and decided that it offered the best cover. We got out and walked past the fitness club. Through the window, I saw rows of red punching bags hanging from the ceiling. Next to that was the weight-lifting area. A boxing ring stood far in the back.

"What now?" Carson asked.

"I'm not going in there, if that's what you're thinking."

"Neither am I. Burger?" Carson asked.

"Sure." At a table with a perfect view of Wade's Jeep, I sipped on my drink while Carson worked on his combo meal.

"This is the longest I've gone without playing baseball."

"I know—it sucks," I said, not offering much hope. "How much time left?"

"Two weeks." Carson played with the straw in his drink. "I was thinking, even when I come back, this steroid thing is going to be on my record and everyone's mind. So maybe it would be better if I switched schools."

"Let's just stay positive." We were starting to wear out our welcome at the burger dive. I couldn't take another dirty look from their crew. After two hours, I was happy to get off the plastic seat and back into my car. We kept the windows down and the music up as we watched Wade's Jeep for activity. Sleepiness started to set in around the three-hour mark.

"What is Wade doing in there?" Carson asked.

"What if he's working out? At three hours, if he's doing this a few times a week, maybe he's not doing steroids."

"My life is officially over." Carson opened his door.

"What are you doing?"

"Finding out what he's doing."

I watched him approach Club 21 Fitness and slip inside. One tense moment turned to five, and the front door finally opened. It was Wade. I turned my car on and when he took off, I pulled up closer to the gym.

Carson burst out the doors and hopped into my car. I zipped onto the street and stayed in the middle lane, looking for Wade.

"There he is!" Carson pointed.

I checked my blind spot before making a sharp turn down a small street. We were about ten car lengths behind him, but it was just the two of us on the road. He made another turn. Then he stopped on the dried-out lawn in front of a green house. I kept driving, hit a dead end and turned around. I parked two houses down from Wade's car.

"Did you know he lived here?" Carson asked.

"No. He never talks about his family at all. I didn't even know this area existed."

We walked toward the house. A sign was dug into the dead lawn that read *Foreclosure. Best deals in town!* A broken wind chime hung by the front door, and a white patterned couch sat on a slab of pavement on the side of the house. A loud noise caught our attention. It was hard to make out the words, but it didn't take long to realize it was a screaming match between a man and a woman.

"We might get a better look if we go to the backyard."

I held out my hand. "After you."

Turning the corner of the house, I spotted something in the dead grass. When it stood up on four legs, I recognized its brown and black fur. A Doberman. It showed its teeth, and I shouted out, "Run!"

I sped to the front of the house and toward the road, Carson close behind me. I could hear the dog snarling and barking in pursuit. It was closing in. I wished I hadn't parked so far away. In full sprint, I pulled my keys out, fumbled and unlocked my car. My door shut just as the Doberman reached me. I quickly unlocked the passenger door for Carson.

He jumped in. "Oh my god! Where's the dog?"

"I don't know!"

I heard a noise, and the dog clawed its way onto my hood. My heart raced as the dog stared me down, slobbering all over my windshield. It was like watching a 3-D movie.

"What are you waiting for? Hit the gas," Carson said, still panicked.

"I'm not going to run over Wade's dog!"

I turned the car on and sprayed some windshield-wiper fluid. It did nothing except jam the wiper blades against the Doberman's giant paws. "Knowing Wade, he probably hasn't fed this thing in a while."

I revved the engine and the dog just stood there, its loud bark penetrating the car. I slid into first gear and inched forward slowly. The Doberman turned like it had heard a noise and took off. "It scratched my car!"

"I would have run it over."

I did my best to ignore Carson and drove slowly up the road. I spotted Wade in front of his house. He was petting the Doberman while screaming at somebody inside. Then Wade slammed the door of his Jeep, leaving his dog behind. I followed Wade all the way to Old Naples, past expensive stores and restaurants. He found street parking close to the beach, and I double-parked. Wade walked past some beachfront homes close to the Naples Pier. Most of them were older bungalows, but because they were on the beach they were probably worth millions. They were all painted bright colors. He turned and walked into a pink bungalow. It was the only home that looked like it was under reconstruction. Parked to the side was a large green Dumpster filled with drywall, broken doors and sheets of metal.

"So all of a sudden Wade's living in a beach house?" Carson asked.

"Looks more like he's slumming it in this fixer-upper." Everything I thought I knew about Wade went out the window. I shrugged my shoulders, more confused than ever.

Chapter Fourteen

Tensions were high as we geared up for a team practice. Rafael had heard that the drug-test results were in. My gut instinct told me that Wade was dealing, working out five days a week and using too. I just hoped the results would nail him. It seemed to take forever for the coaches to arrive.

Coach Brigman wasted no time. "I can't express to you guys how much it hurt to think that you were messing around with drugs." He cleared his throat. "I've lost sleep over this test and what it means to this school. The results are in..."

I looked at Wade. He stood there looking confident, even sporting a slight smirk.

"Well, imagine my surprise," the coach said, "when you all came back clean!"

The Sharks, minus me, cheered loudly.

"I'm proud of you boys."

Everyone high-fived. I wondered what they were thinking. Were they happy they didn't get caught or relieved that Wade didn't frame them like he did Carson?

"Now it's time to refocus on baseball and look ahead. This year's Blue Diamond Skills Showcase event was supposed to be at Bonita Bay. But because they only have one diamond and the signup for this event is bigger than expected...it's going to be held here."

Again, the Sharks cheered.

"As in years past," Coach Brigman said, "you can expect college scouts to attend. The events are laid out on both fields. I will be on the bigger field and Santos and

McKay will be on the smaller field. Today, I want you to make sure you get to each spot. We have fastest ninety feet, longest toss, three-man relay, pitcher accuracy and home-run derby. Have fun and give it your all."

Everyone jumped to it. I wasn't in such a rush, feeling defeated with the whole Wade situation. I made my way toward the second field, hoping to avoid him for a while. Coach Santos stood at home plate. It was just me, Adrian and Tom. They were probably happy to get away from Wade too.

Coach Santos got our attention. "Fielding, arm strength and hitting ability are some of the things college coaches are looking for. And then there's speed."

He paused. I wondered if he was upset that only three of us had chosen him first.

"In my opinion, this is one skill that can help separate you from the pack." He stepped on home plate and took a swing with an invisible bat. "Ninety feet could be what's standing in your way to college ball."

"What speed are they looking for?" Tom asked.

"Great question. Mickey Mantle played for the Yankees in the 1950s and '60s. He was able to run from home to first in three-point-one seconds. If you can do it in four seconds, coaches will salivate over you. Four-point-four seconds is considered average. Who's ready to try the ninety-foot dash?"

Tom was first to jump at the opportunity, even though he had three more years before he had to worry about this. Coach Santos showed him the stopwatch, and Tom didn't look pleased.

I stepped to home plate. Some loud oohs and ahhs echoed from the main field. I was certain that Wade was knocking them out of the park. When it finally died down, Coach Santos held up his stopwatch and gave me the thumbs-up. I pushed off the plate. Then, halfway to first, Wade popped into my head and I bailed on my first attempt.

When it was my turn again, I told the coach that I needed to stretch more. I was really just buying time to wipe Wade from my mind. Adrian and Tom ran twice more, and I had done all the stalling I could do. I was just getting my focus back when Wade showed up.

"What's the time to beat?" he asked.

"Five seconds."

Adrian and Tom cleared out, replaced by Wade, Darren and some other followers.

"Let's do this," Wade announced.

Coach Santos must've sensed that I was off my game, because he offered everyone some pointers. "Keep your head up, elbows in and shoulders slightly forward. Toes should be straight, and you want a pumping motion with your arms. The faster they go back and forth, the faster your feet will move."

It was a lot to think about. With my eyes locked on first base, I took off. I passed Wade and Darren and they said something to try and distract me, but I couldn't make it out. Halfway there, I felt like I was really hitting my stride. Arms pumping, I propelled myself forward, hit first base and started to fall. I was out of control. I hit the grass and rolled a few times.

Back on my feet, grass stains and all, I hurried to Coach Santos. He held up the stopwatch: *4.3*. I was a sliver better than average.

Wade jumped onto home plate, ready to go. He had a faster takeoff than I did, gracefully blowing past first base. I could tell from Coach Santos's stunned reaction that the college coaches would be drooling over Wade.

At the end of practice, I sat with my back to the outfield fence and finished my jug of water. It was nice to sit in the late-day shade, but I was really avoiding the team. Everyone would be getting changed in the locker room, and Wade would be boasting about his record-breaking outing. When I saw most of the team heading to the parking lot, I moved to the locker room to grab my backpack. I could hear my phone beeping in my bag. Then a voice behind me made me spin around.

It was Tom.

"Hey."

"Just so you know, Griffin, I was here."

I looked at him, waiting for clarification. When I didn't get any, I said, "Okay. I'm here too."

"Nothing happened."

"Are you okay, Tom?"

"People fall all the time."

Had Wade finally cracked him, or was it heat stroke?

"So you can go and report what you want, but no one's going to believe you."

What was this? Was he threatening me?

"You know, Tom, I always thought you'd rise above Wade...stand up for yourself." I grabbed my backpack, but when I turned back around, Tom was gone. Wade was standing in his place.

"Your monkey...I mean, dog, just left."

"Griff, this could've been the year for you."

"What do you want?"

He stepped closer. "I had a lot of respect for you. Even thought we'd both go to U of Miami. Play ball for the Hurricanes."

"Well, things don't always go the way we plan." *Was he fishing for an apology?*

He wasn't going to get one after everything he'd done.

He continued to stare at me.

"It's been nice. I gotta go." My phone beeped again. When I reached for it, Wade's fist appeared in front of my face. He slugged me on my right cheekbone, and I went down like a featherweight.

Chapter Fifteen

The smell and taste of blood kicked in as I did my best to break my fall. Sprawled out and at eye level with Wade's baseball cleats, I quickly reviewed my options. I could fight this animal pumped up on 'roids, or I could make a run for it.

The choice was obvious.

I got to my knees, and Wade was ready to deliver another blow. I stood, wiped some blood from my lip and broke into a sprint. Halfway to the door he tackled me.

I tried to struggle free, but he pinned my hands down.

He was seething. "You think you can take me on?"

The more I tried to escape, the more he pressed his weight down on me. I twisted my arms and wrists around. That didn't work, so I tried to push my waist up, hoping to bounce him off me. He was too heavy.

He smiled, staring down at me. "Helpless now, right?"

I hoped he'd realize that he'd proven his point and just let me go. The more I laid there, the harder it became to breathe. "You win, Wade."

"Are you even listening to me? You brought this on yourself."

I was out of options and somehow making him even madder. I couldn't take him staring down at me anymore. One last-ditch, Hail Mary plan came to me. I used my tongue to draw in as much bloody saliva as I could and spat it at him.

Wade let go of my right arm to wipe it away, and I used my free arm to elbow him off me. I jumped to my feet, grabbed my backpack and ran as hard as I could. I must've beat Mickey Mantle's record. In my car, I screeched out of the parking lot and didn't stop driving until I made it to the closest mall. I parked in front of Target and looked at my face in the rearview mirror. I had a swollen bloody lip. There was no sign of Wade. I grabbed my backpack and used the restroom to clean up. I glanced at my phone and saw that there was a text from Carson.

I'm @ support group. Derek squealed!

I didn't sleep all night and did my best to hide from my dad, telling him I was cramming for a big test. I blew through school, making sure to dodge Carson and to take my lunch off-site. It wasn't until last class that he finally found me.

"It's over," I told Carson. "I can't help you anymore."

"What happened to your face?"

I thought back to Tom's warning the night before. "I fell," I said sarcastically.

121

"Did you get my text?" Carson asked. "Derek went right to Wade and told him everything we said."

"Doesn't matter. Wade wins. We lose. Game over." I brushed past him to my seat. I had much bigger concerns. I was scheduled to work that afternoon, and I was scared that Wade was too. I thought about calling in sick, but I needed the money.

I was first out the door at the bell. When I got to the golf club, I circled the parking lot for fifteen minutes, looking for Wade's Jeep. Maybe my luck was turning around... for today at least.

My boss, some college kid, assigned me to bag drop-off.

I stood under a green tarp and greeted members as they returned from an afternoon of golf. I tried to act cheerful even though I wasn't in the mood.

After an hour and a half, I was moved to the golf-cart drop-off area. Adrian worked the shed, and I did my best to keep up the small talk. Even though my top lip hurt, I continued to force a smile for tips. One out of every twenty people would ask about my injury. Most of them would joke about me losing a fight, and I played along.

Two carts rolled in, and I recognized one of the players. The man with thinning blond hair pulled into a ponytail and serious muscles was Wade's uncle Jim.

"How was the game?" I asked him.

"Be careful with the clubs," he said. Then he walked off without even looking at me.

"Just like Wade," I muttered. I pulled the clubs off the cart and handed them to Adrian. I slammed on the gas and whipped the cart around the corner and into the recharging bay. They had left the cart a mess, with empty cans of beer and half-eaten sandwiches. I tossed them into the bin and started to clear out the back basket. At the bottom was a driver cover. I brought it back to the front and asked Adrian to switch jobs with me.

"Why?" he said.

"Because. Just do it."

Adrian's attention turned over my shoulder. "Check out the awesome car."

I turned to see Uncle Jim drive off in a gleaming yellow Porsche with the roof down.

"Sweet ride. You know how much those babies cost?"

"Yeah." My dad's dream was to sell Porsches. "Over a hundred thousand dollars, fully loaded."

"Man, I need to play for the major leagues."

"That guy"—I held up the cover—"left this here. Show me where you put his clubs."

"I can take it for you."

"Just show me." I followed Adrian into the shed, and he stopped in front of the clubs. They were on the second shelf. "Switch with me. Cover the front."

"You sure?"

"Yeah, you deserve to make tips too."

"Thanks, Griffin. Wade was wrong about—" He stopped midsentence, looking embarrassed. "Thanks."

He took off and I pulled the set of clubs down. I found the driver that was missing its cover and put it back on. I thought about what Adrian had said and how Wade was badmouthing me to the rest of the team. For all the times he'd stolen from members' golf bags, I should have reported him. I hoisted the golf bag, steadied it on the shelf and paused. I brought it back down, checked to see that no one was around and started going through the pockets. I didn't even know what I was looking for. The first pocket had a golf glove and a dollar bill. I left it. A long zippered pocket had a rain jacket and a couple of old scorecards. The next section had golf balls, tees, ball markers, a small towel and a divot repairer. I pulled out the towel to get a closer look and saw that it was rolled up and secured by two elastic bands.

I checked over my shoulder and could hear Adrian talking to a guest. He was probably wondering why I hadn't come out to put away the clubs.

I pulled the elastic bands off and unraveled the towel. Inside were several ziplock sandwich bags, and each had about twenty small pills. Some were green and white gel capsules without any markings. Others were white pills with writing. On one side, they had an italicized *W* in a box. The other side had the letter *D* over the number thirty-seven. I snapped some pictures with my phone, making sure to get the membership-number tag in the shot.

I didn't know what the pills were for, so I decided to do some research on my break. The gel capsules looked a lot like the steroid pics, although without markings it was hard to be sure. I did find the white pill though. It was Demerol—a kind of pain-killer. The website said it was a narcotic, and there was a big warning that it was a habit-forming drug.

Maybe Wade's uncle had chronic pain or something. But why would he carry so many pills with him, hidden away in a towel? Hadn't he heard of a bottle? I thought back to his argument with Wade and wondered if there was any connection.

Chapter Sixteen

I waited impatiently for Carson at his locker. When he showed up, I grabbed him, maybe a little too forcefully, and hauled him to the closest restroom.

"What's your problem?"

I banged the base of my fist on each stall door, opening them to make sure no one was around.

"Paranoid much?" Carson asked.

"We can't trust anyone."

Carson's eyes lit up. "What do you know?"

"I am not exactly sure how all the dots connect." I checked the entrance one more time. "Wade's using and dealing. He's living in a dilapidated shack soon to be taken by some bank. Yet somehow he has access to a beach house." I was on a roll. "I saw his uncle Jim at the club and found out that he's hiding drugs in his golf bag." I held out one of the pictures I'd taken on my phone.

Carson nodded his head, deep in thought. "What really happened to your face?"

"That's not the point!"

"So you didn't fall?"

"Wade hit me," I said, my voice rising louder than I meant it to. "He attacked me because he knew about Derek."

"We can report this! You're the proof!"

"Trust me," I said. "The answer's no. Can we focus?"

"Okay."

"Back to what I was saying. I think Wade's hiding the drugs he sells in his uncle's golf bag."

"Who would think to look there?"

"Exactly."

"So we need to talk to his uncle Jim."

"Are you kidding?" I said. "Have you seen him?"

"So then what?"

There was a moment of silence. "What if Wade's not working alone?" I said finally.

"Someone on the team?"

I nodded.

Carson smiled. "Sounds like we're doing a shakedown."

At lunch, I sat with Carson while we ate a couple of burritos. We used a napkin to draw the Sharks depth chart. Each Shark was placed at his position on the crudely drawn diamond. "So who do you want to go after?" I asked.

"My first choice is Darren, but that would just be stupid."

"Then I say we go after Wade's dogs."

Carson placed his hand over his chest. "Please. You know how much I hate that term."

I bought Carson some churros to cheer him up. The hard part, I figured, would be to find a way to scare them into ratting on Wade.

After lunch, we found Adrian in the science lab.

He glanced up from his experiment and didn't look pleased to see us.

"We need to talk," I said.

"Can't. This science experiment is due today."

"For?" I asked.

"Not Wade, if that's what you're thinking."

I pointed. "That pale yellow substance is sulfuric acid. You add that sugar and mix it, better look out."

Adrian looked at me.

"You're about to make a dangerous mixture called the black snake. The sugar will turn black and then it will grow out of the beaker, creating sulfur dioxide. Not only will it stink, but it can be dangerous too."

Adrian stepped back.

"You wouldn't know because you're in grade nine, but that's the grade-twelve properties-of-substances assignment. Not only is Wade's chem assignment late, but it's also seriously dangerous."

"Okay, fine. What do we need to talk about?" Adrian said.

Carson had insisted on a good cop, bad cop routine. "I'm worried about you, Adrian." I was the good cop.

"What's wrong?" he asked, still avoiding eye contact.

"What's wrong?" Carson spewed back. "Don't play the innocent card."

Carson's act was a bit over the top. We weren't trying to scare Adrian away.

"You're going down for the crime, my friend," he carried on. Carson was definitely watching too many crime shows.

"What are you guys talking about?"

I needed to step in. "Please, just ask yourself—is it worth the risk of losing everything?"

"What risk?"

"Oh, I don't know...the risk of you losing your spot on the team, graduating high school...and that's just the start."

"Guys, you're freaking me out. So if this is a joke, ha-ha."

"The only one laughing is Wade," Carson said. "He's using you."

"So this is about Wade?" Adrian looked me square in the face. "He's the captain of the team. I hate to say it, but everyone looks up to him. Not you."

We weren't going to crack him. It was time to wrap this up.

"Good luck—you're going to need it," I said, leading Carson out of the lab.

When we were out of earshot, I pulled Carson aside. "No more good cop, bad cop."

"Yeah, that was a total bomb."

"Atomic."

Chapter Seventeen

The next day, we found Tom in the library over lunch hour. We pulled up two chairs and sat next to him. I figured that if we couldn't find out the truth, we'd just make it up.

"Tom, put the homework down. We know what you've been doing."

He looked more confused than Adrian had.

I raised my voice just above the acceptable library volume. "We know you're the one on the team that's using drugs. And that you're selling them too."

"What? No!"

I stood and led him to the cover of the stacks. "I have proof."

"I don't use drugs."

"Then who does?"

He paused. "No one that I know."

"You're a liar and I can prove it." I walked back to the table and grabbed his backpack. I started to empty it. Books, pencils and a calculator flooded the table. Then, from a small zipped pocket in the front, I pulled out a plastic bag of white pills. "What are these then?"

I thought he was going to have a heart attack right then and there. Too bad he didn't know they were just a few aspirin that Carson had planted seconds before. "You get caught with these and you have no future."

"I didn't know what to do."

Carson and I exchanged a look. "What do you mean?"

Tom looked genuinely upset. His face was red like he was about to cry. "Nothing."

"We can help you, Tom. You're not alone."

"Okay, fine." He paused. "But we'll have to skip final period."

I nodded.

At two thirty, Carson and I met Tom in the parking lot.

"Where to?" I asked.

He looked around like someone might be watching him. Then he took off in a light sprint around the side of the school. He passed the basketball courts and walked toward the baseball diamond. He moved along the outfield fence and stopped at the 250-yard sign. "This is it."

"Is this a trick? Is Wade waiting for us?"

"You said you'd help."

"Okay, yes, we will. We trust you."

Tom reached above the sign to the padding that outlined the top of the outfield fence.

He lifted up a section of the padding to reveal a slender silver box attached to the metal bar with a magnet.

"What's that?" Carson asked.

I answered for him. "Drugs." I took the silver box and slid open the lid. Inside were green and white capsules and a handful of white pills just like the ones I'd seen in Wade's uncle Jim's golf bag.

"Flip it over," Tom said.

The back had a magnet glued to it and a name cut into it. *Tom.*

"How did you know about this?" I asked Tom.

"I don't trust Wade. I followed him one day."

Tom grabbed the box back from me. "We need to get out of here."

"Why don't you just take it?" Carson asked.

"Because he'll know. He said he'd kill—"

"You?"

"No. My dog." Tom looked at me. "So, how are you going to help me?"

I thought about it for a minute, wanting to give him a good answer. "At baseball practice tomorrow, tell him I forced you to show this to me."

"Are you crazy?" Carson said.

I shrugged. "Time will tell."

Chapter Eighteen

At practice, I had one eye on Tom and the other on Carson. From the steps of the stands, Carson aimed his phone at Wade. It felt great to know that I finally had dirt on Wade. I just needed to seal the deal with proof.

The Sharks warmed up without a clue that drugs were hidden on the outfield fence. I had to admit, it was a brilliant hiding spot.

Wade tossed a ball with Rafael in the outfield. It didn't take long for Tom to interrupt, pull Wade aside and tell him that I knew where the drugs were hidden.

I was smiling behind my glove as Tom broke the news. The reaction on Wade's face made my heart skip a beat. He turned to me, and I quickly looked away.

Wade joined two others in the outfield.

"That's it," I said under my breath, "go check on your stash." I watched him in the outfield. He was in the vicinity of the 250 marker but couldn't get enough privacy to do a quick check. He surprised me and moved along the outfield fence toward the gate. Were there more containers? Maybe they had all our names on them, like insurance plans. Then I saw his uncle Jim at the gate. Wade approached him, and they immediately broke into an argument.

I waved Carson over and inched toward them to get a better look. Wade seemed to be pleading with his uncle.

They walked through the gate and out of sight. I rushed to the parking lot and made it in time to see two men appear and grab Wade.

Panicked, I ran toward Wade as he tried to struggle free. Before I could get there, they tossed him into the open door of a black Escalade SUV and drove off.

Still in shock, I spotted Carson next to me, phone in hand.

I reached for my keys but forgot that I was in my uniform. "My keys are in my pants in the change room. Get my car and find me. Tell the coaches I don't feel well and you're driving me home."

"But I've only got my learner's license."

"Run!"

I ran as hard as I could through the gate and past the basketball courts. When I got to the main parking lot, I spotted the SUV driving down Shark Way. The red brake lights came on as they neared the stop sign. I remembered that there was a large median on Immokalee Road. They had to go right.

I bolted down Shark Way and turned right. With no sign of Carson, I didn't know what to do, so I kept running.

Up ahead, red brake lights caught my attention again. The SUV was making a left at the stoplight. I checked for traffic and darted across to the median.

When the SUV's left turn became a U-turn, I backtracked along the median. Now the SUV was heading toward me. I knew Jim would see me, sticking out from the scenery in my baseball uniform. There was a small palm tree, barely taller than I was. I ducked down next to it, hiding among the bushes lined up on either side of the tree.

The SUV passed, and I turned. I was out of steam. My only hope was Carson.

I jumped up when I saw my Mustang puttering along the side of the road. It took forever for a truck to pass so that I could get safely into my car. I leaped into the passenger seat, startling Carson. "Make a U-turn!"

Carson gripped the steering wheel. I watched as he painstakingly checked and rechecked the driver's side and rearview mirrors.

"Come on, come on...let's roll!"

My car screeched as Carson put it into first gear.

"Clutch, then release with gas."

He struggled to shift out of first.

"They're getting away. Get out." He pulled over and we switched spots. "You drive worse than an old man." After making a U-turn at the light, we drove in silence for a couple of miles.

Carson was first to talk. "I aced my DMV test."

"Doesn't matter now. They got away." I could feel his eyes on me. "Sorry. It's not your fault."

The tension in the car started to ease up.

Carson had his phone out. "I think we should call the cops."

"And what would we say to them?"

"Good point."

We did another mile in silence. The only sound was the replay of Wade and Jim's argument coming from Carson's phone. "His uncle Jim looks like a wrestler," Carson said.

We both looked at each other. "The gym!"

My stomach dropped when I didn't see the SUV near the entrance of Club 21 Fitness. Then I spotted it parked in the far corner of the lot. It looked empty. We decided our only option was to go into the gym.

We walked through the front doors, scanning the room. To our left were rows of rubber torsos on stands. A large man was knocking the plastic brains out of one rubber man. To our right was a large collection of weight-lifting equipment.

An incredibly fit woman greeted us at the front desk. "How can I help you?"

Carson was silent. It was up to me. "Can we check out a membership?"

"Sure. Let me get somebody—"

"Actually, do you mind if we just look around first?"

She smiled. Her teeth were white and perfectly straight. "Sure. Let me know when you're ready."

I avoided the scary-looking dudes pumping weights and walked into an open area with a boxing ring.

"She's cute."

"Carson, can we focus?"

He nodded.

I pointed to a set of doors with a sign that read *Employees Only*.

"Act like you belong," I whispered.

We passed through the doors into a small warehouse. There were a few desks and lots of boxes. An open box nearby was filled with bottles labeled *Raptor-Xtreme bodybuilding supplement*.

I continued to lead Carson through the zigzag of boxes. Then my stomach hit the floor. I spotted Wade sitting on a chair, surrounded by Jim and his two sidekicks. I could see that Wade's hands were tied behind his back. I was beginning to doubt that Jim was Wade's real uncle.

I pulled back to safety.

Carson whispered, "Can we call the cops now?"

I eyed a phone sitting on a desk. It took a while to figure out that I had to press Line 1 and then the number nine to get a dial tone. I dialed 9-1-1 and whispered, "Emergency...Club 21 Fitness...Jim," to the person on the other end and then gently placed the phone back down.

Carson's hands were shaking. "We need to leave."

I shook my head and led Carson to cover behind a row of shelves.

Jim stood over Wade, pointing his finger. "I keep giving you chance after chance to pay."

"A few more days," Wade said, pulling on his restraints.

"And what did I say I'd do if you didn't get the money?"

Wade struggled to break free.

"That's right. How are you going to play baseball if you're injured?"

"Where are the cops?" I said.

Carson insisted, "We need to go."

As scared as I was, leaving Wade was not an option. "We need to distract them. Can you do that?"

Carson took off. After a few moments of silence, I started to wonder if he was going to come back. Then I heard the photocopy machine come to life.

So did Jim. "You two, go see what that's all about."

I ducked behind a desk and the two hulks walked past me. *Where is Carson?*

"Boss, check this out."

My heart sank. *Did they catch him?*

"Someone's running nine hundred copies... of their butt cheeks."

"What?!" Jim hustled past me to have a look. I stood and felt a tap on my shoulder. When I turned, I was relieved to see Carson. We hurried over to Wade.

Wade's eyes went wide. He looked like he was in shock. "Griff? What are you doing here?"

I quickly ripped the tape off his wrists and ankles. "We've gotta get you out of here."

"Follow me," Wade said. "I know another way out."

We ducked around the boxes, heading in the opposite direction from Jim. The back door came into view, and I could almost taste the fresh air. Then a golf driver sliced through the air in front of me. I skidded to a stop and Carson bumped into me, almost knocking me over.

Jim stepped out from behind a stack of boxes.

Wade didn't hesitate, breaking sharply to the left.

I tried to keep up with Wade, but he was moving too fast. Within seconds I was lost and out of breath.

"There's no escape!" Jim called out.

I stood doubled over at the waist, trying to slow down my breathing. I was surprised to hear Wade's voice. "Don't hurt them—they don't know anything."

"Fine with me. Show yourself and they can go out the back."

"All right. Guys, it's okay," Wade said. "Come on out."

I peeked around the corner. Wade was standing at a distance from Jim and the two men. One of them held the back door open.

Each step I took was one step closer to escaping this hell. I saw Carson come out from the shadows. *He's your younger cousin. Carson goes out first.* When we got to the door, I gestured for Carson to go ahead of me. Then, out of nowhere, someone pushed me forward. I fell into the goon holding the door, taking him and Carson down with me. When I looked up, all I could see was Wade, out in the back parking lot, running for his life. Then the door slammed shut.

Chapter Nineteen

"Wade!" I screamed his name until I thought my ears might bleed.

Jim signaled and one of his goons took off after Wade. The other goon handed Jim a piece of paper. It was a photocopy of Carson's butt. Jim held it out to us and shook his head. Normally, I would have laughed.

I eyed the door and tried to calculate the odds of making it out alive. But I wasn't going to ditch Carson. My mind raced for ways to escape, and I kept coming back to that door.

"I didn't know Wade had friends," Jim said, a sinister smile on his face.

I wasn't sure what Jim had planned for us. I screamed as loud as I could.

Carson started screaming too. Then our voices were joined by a louder sound.

Police sirens.

I had almost forgotten that we'd called the police. *Thank you, Carson*!

Jim looked at his goon in disbelief. "Seriously?"

The PA crackled and a woman announced, "Mr. Muller, you are needed at the front desk."

The weight of the goon keeping me down made it challenging to breathe. "They're going to be looking for me."

"You called?"

The PA squawked again. This time the voice was more urgent. "Mr. Muller, you are needed at the front desk."

"And what if I call your bluff?" Jim asked.

I stared back at him.

The voice on the PA broke the standoff. It asked for Jim again, this time adding the words "Collier County Police."

Jim, in a frustrated voice, barked, "Get him up."

On my feet, I struggled to breathe normally.

Jim let out a long sigh. "Open it."

A goon opened the door.

I told Carson to go first, and when I went to follow, Jim stepped in my way.

"Stupid move, putting yourself on the line for a loser like Wade."

I didn't say anything. He moved out of my way.

"Guess we'll be seeing you around. You talk to those cops, you and your family will regret it."

I stepped through the door and into the early-evening air. It felt cool and fresh.

Carson said, "Wade's got a really nice uncle."

"He's not his real uncle, you know."

"I know—just joking."

We moved around to the front of the building and saw a police car with flashing lights. I wanted to go talk to them, maybe see Jim taken out in handcuffs. Then I remembered his threat. I fumbled for my keys and started the car.

"What are you going to tell your dad, Griff?"

"I don't know. What about you?"

He shrugged.

"I think there's someone else we need to talk to first."

The next day, Wade was a no-show at school. That wasn't going to stop us. When we got to Coach Brigman's office, I could tell he wasn't thrilled to see us. How could I blame him? Last time Carson and I had news, he had to drug-test his entire team, and everyone came back clean.

"What's up, boys? Carson, I hope you're on the path to recovery."

"Coach, Carson has never done steroids."

"I appreciate your perseverance—"

I cut him off, smiling. "But we know who does."

"You need proof."

Carson jumped in. "Wade's been hazing people on the team. He's selling and using steroids."

"And he's getting the drugs from this guy called Uncle Jim," I said.

"I'm taking what you're saying seriously, but can you back it up?"

I texted Tom, and within a few minutes he had joined us in the office. We took the coach to the outfield fence and showed him Wade's secret stash.

Coach Brigman was speechless.

Chapter Twenty

Carson called me repeatedly, despite the fact that he knew I was at work. I couldn't take my phone vibrating anymore, so I finally answered.

"I know Coach said he'd handle things from here," Carson blurted out, "but if we hadn't taken charge, nothing would have changed."

"What's your point?"

"Aren't you mad at Wade for tricking us at the gym?"

"Yes."

"And I know Wade will probably be cut from the team, but I'm still mad. Plus, we know where Wade is hiding out."

"The beach house." After a double shift at the golf club, I had my sights on a turkey sandwich and the Miami Marlins versus Atlanta Braves game at home. But this was important. "I'll pick you up."

The late Saturday crowd was starting to thin out at the beach. Carson and I walked the perimeter of the house, looking for a way in. The sliding glass door off the beach was the best option. I pushed on the handle, and the door glided open. I lifted a curtain and stepped in cautiously.

"This place is disgusting."

I covered my nose. There was no furniture, and most of the drywall was torn down. "How can Wade stay here?" The kitchen was lined with half-eaten cans of food. I turned the tap, and dirty liquid spat out.

"Look." Carson pointed.

A toilet sat in a closet. "That's where the smell's coming from." I spun around at the sound of the sliding door opening. Wade stood there, staring back at me. For a second, I thought he was going to run. Instead, he came in and dropped his backpack on a plastic patio table.

"Want a drink?"

I thought about the sink and shook my head.

He grabbed a bottled water and said, "Here" before throwing one at Carson.

Carson plucked it from the air. "Thanks."

It was the most the two of them had spoken in weeks.

After a long, uncomfortable silence, Wade lowered his water bottle. "I was just trying to make some money for college. Otherwise, how is a guy like me going to get there? And local college? Their baseball teams suck in comparison."

It was unexpected, but I actually started to feel bad for Wade.

"I don't have it like you guys."

Then I remembered how he'd deserted us at the gym. "You could have gotten me killed! How could you take off like that?"

"Look, I don't know how to make this up to you. You shouldn't have rescued me. I didn't ask for your help. And now, again, you're here. Stop tracking me down. I don't have anything for you. So why don't you two just leave? Now!"

We didn't budge. He wasn't getting off that easy.

Carson exploded with anger. "You took me down and ruined my baseball career." His face was getting redder. "You're not going to get away with something like that."

"Carson, you're a smarter guy than me."

I didn't expect that to come from Wade's mouth.

"And if you don't end up playing baseball, you'll become a doctor or something. I have no options. No backup plan. There's no mommy or daddy helping out. Get it?"

We didn't answer.

"No scholarship for me means no future." Wade stopped and took a chug of water.

"I know that doesn't make sense to you, but if you saw where I grew up, maybe it might. So, I'm sorry for wanting to wipe out my competition."

I never thought I'd see the day when Wade apologized. It didn't matter now though. An apology from him was empty. Useless.

"If that's what you're here for, then take it."

"Wade, that's not going to be good enough—" I stopped and turned toward a loud thud coming from the front door. It struck again, this time sending the door down and revealing Jim and his goons.

Jim smiled and took a calculated step into the house. "I want my money." He sniffed and signaled for his goons to follow him. "You're also going to pay me back for my bail."

I met Carson's gaze and knew exactly what he was thinking. He bolted and I followed him through the gap in the sliding door. We hit the boardwalk, running like mad. A quick look over my shoulder revealed Wade gaining on us. He was holding his backpack in his arms like a football. Behind him, Jim and his two buddies were in pursuit. A few more strides and Wade overtook us. I guess pumping steroids comes in handy when being chased by people who want you dead.

Wade turned onto the pier, and without thinking, Carson and I followed him. Big mistake. We were heading toward a dead end. Dim streetlights lined the pier. I did my best not to trip on the uneven wooden planks. The farther I ran down the pier, the higher the drop to the water became.

"Stop!" Jim screamed.

Wade stopped, so I did too, about halfway up the pier.

"Give me the backpack," Jim said.

Wade moved to the edge of the walkway, grabbing onto the wooden rail.

What's he up to? I didn't know if he was going to jump or pull out a gun.

Wade leaped onto the ledge.

"Think about what you're doing."

I didn't know what to do, so I joined Wade on the ledge, figuring I was probably going to have to jump. I helped Carson up, trying not to fall. I noticed the last rays of the sun dip down. I turned to the board-walk to find just a few stragglers. "Help! Please help!" They ignored me, probably thinking I was some strung-out teen.

"Come on, Wade." Jim held out his hands, palms up. "Don't make a bad mistake. Step down so we can talk."

Wade held the backpack off the pier. "Step closer and I'll drop the money."

In the dark, I couldn't see how far the drop down to the water was. Other than the slight glint off the whitecaps, it was total blackness. I could swim no problem. But could I survive the fall?

Chapter Twenty-One

Jim's goons took a step toward us.

"Jump?" Carson asked.

"Not yet." I looked at Wade. He didn't look scared. He actually looked like he was enjoying being the one in control.

"You know, Jim," Wade said, "you deserve this." Wade released his grip on the backpack, and it fell from sight. Jim ran to the ledge to track it while both goons swandived off the ledge.

Not wasting time, I grabbed Carson and we jumped flat-footed onto the pier. Then we ran. Wade overtook both of us, and we stuck close by him. I glanced over my shoulder, but there was no sign of Jim. Wade tried to lose us by darting into a gelato restaurant. I found him sitting at a booth with his eyes glued to the window. He nearly jumped when Carson and I sat down across from him.

"You're insane, Wade." A waitress came by, and we told her we needed a minute. "And why would you throw money into the water? It's just going to make Jim even madder."

Wade smiled and discreetly lifted the bottom of his T-shirt, exposing wads of cash wrapped in ziplock bags.

"You're going to get yourself killed. Why keep Jim's money?"

"You ask too many questions."

"Can you be honest for once in your life?"

Wade lowered his voice. "He's the one who came up to me while I was working out. It started with a sampling of steroids, like we were buddies and he was just trying to help me. Next thing I know, I'm out drumming up business at school for him. The harder I worked for that guy, the more he thought he had me in his back pocket, and the less he paid me. So what's so wrong with skimming a little cash to take care of my future? No one else is."

I didn't have the guts to tell him that the coach knew everything. "And now what?"

"You two have a gelato. I'm out of here."

As he left, I wondered if I was ever going to see him again.

My dad wasn't pleased to find out about my recent adventures, but telling him was the right thing to do. Plus, I knew he'd be getting a phone call from the coach, the principal or both. At first he was upset, but the skills event was a great conversation changer.

"Everybody listen up." I stood on the bench in the dugout. The skills event was about to start, and there was a definite buzz of excitement in the air. "I know you are all wondering what's up with Wade."

"Who cares what you have to say?" Darren shouted.

"Fine then—*you* update everybody."

He looked at me, clueless.

"Figured that. Unlike Darren, I saw Wade yesterday. Today, he's a no-show." I waited for a reaction but didn't get any. "Carson can confirm all of what I'm about to say."

Carson nodded. I could tell he was happy to be back on the team.

"First, I'm going to lay down some new rules. The freshmen will no longer be referred to as dogs. Just Sharks, like the rest of us. Wade's hazing and homework programs are officially canceled."

The team reacted as I expected. Even though Wade was probably fifty miles away, on the run from Jim, they were still scared of him. "I spoke to Wade last night, and he's got bigger problems right now than baseball."

"It's true," Carson added. "Wade's in over his head."

"So, there are two rules on this team. First, play as a team for once. And second, play to win. If you don't like the rules, you can leave."

Darren sneered. "You're not the captain."

"Speaking of that," I said, "Coach asked us to pick a new one. All in favor of me, raise your hands."

Tom and Adrian were the first to raise their hands. Almost everyone else followed.

"Done." I put my Sharks hat on. "Time to focus on impressing the scouts."

Coach Brigman entered the dugout. "Mind if I jump in?"

I stepped down, and he patted me on the back. "Thanks, Griff. We all want to impress the college scouts. They're going to be looking for a lot of skill sets, but the big one is hustle. Sharks, let's give them an intensity that will leave an impression. So get out—"

Coach Brigman stopped midsentence, his eyes fixed on the field behind us. I didn't have to turn around to know it was Wade. *How dumb can he be?* He was standing there in uniform.

Darren smiled knowingly at me.

"Ready to play, Coach," Wade said.

"We're going to need to talk first." Coach Brigman told us to go out and have fun, then turned his attention to Wade.

Everyone hit the field, but I took my time, watching Coach McKay and Coach Santos surround Wade. The field was filled with different colored jerseys representing the other schools. Spectators walked by with hot dogs and cotton candy. There was so much commotion, but all I could focus on was Wade being escorted off the field. He had screwed up big-time, and he deserved this. Still, I wondered how he felt. Did he have a clue that it was over for him?

After a few warm-ups, I waited in line against the fence for the fastest-ninety-feet event. When my turn came, I stepped onto home plate. My dad waved from the stands, and I smiled back. A coach from another team held up his stopwatch and gave me the thumbs-up. *Put it all behind you. Time to move on.* With bent knees and my leadoff arm out, I took off. I kept my head down and pushed forward, forcing my legs to take longer strides. Near the halfway mark, I felt my arms and legs moving as one, helping to increase my speed. I stormed down the baseline and blasted past first base. I kept running, taking my time before turning around. I rolled back to first, catching my breath, and spotted two scouts talking over a clipboard. They were watching me. I figured that everyone was probably desperate to know their speed. I walked past as one scout held up the stopwatch. "No thanks, I'm good."

"You sure?"

I'd done the best I could. A number wouldn't change that. "Yup."

"Like your attitude!"

I turned, looking for Carson, but bumped into a spectator wearing a Miami Marlins hat and sunglasses. "Sorry about that." When I looked up, I saw it was Jim.

Chapter Twenty-Two

He had a fake smile plastered on his face. I looked but couldn't spot his right and left wingmen.

Other than at the golf club, this was the only time I'd seen Jim without them.

"What a great day for baseball!"

I examined his poorly planned disguise. No hat or reflective sunglasses could camouflage his wrestler's body. "I don't know where Wade is."

"My friend, I'm not interested in Wade."

Friend?

"I'm a big enough man to cut my losses and set my sights on new ventures."

"And I could scream for help and then what?"

"No need. You're busy here. I can see that this is an important day in your life. Just one more thing for now."

I scanned the horizon over Jim's shoulders. *Where was Carson?*

"I could use a smart young man like you."

"That what you said to Wade?"

"Wade makes me out to be the bad guy here, but I didn't force him into doing anything. Let's remember that it was him who stole from me."

"Jim, I'm not interested."

"Don't you hate it when people can't see a good deal staring them in the face? A couple hours a week, helping people with their problems, and you'd be set. No part-time jobs, student loans...you'd get to call the shots."

I had an imaginary flashback to what it must've been like for Wade. Promises of big money. Maybe a free gym membership and an opportunity to bulk up. Wade stuck living in that horrible house...I couldn't say I was surprised that he'd turned to a guy like Jim. *Uncle Jim.*

"Why don't you think it over?"

"No. Not a chance."

"Okay, you drive a hard bargain. Let's go for a drive and I'll sweeten the deal."

"Please leave me—"

"I'm not asking." Jim grabbed my arm forcefully. I tried to break free, but his grip tightened on my elbow.

Jim smiled at a passerby, rustling my hair with his free hand. "That's it. Keep moving."

"Packing it in already, Griff?" Coach Brigman was headed our way.

"You the coach?" Jim asked.

"Yes, and who are you?"

Jim released his grip, pressing his hand into my shoulder. "I'm his uncle."

I looked at the coach. *Come on, don't buy this.*

"We'll be right back. I have a present in my car." Jim lowered his voice, but I could still hear. "It's a brand-new Rawlings baseball glove."

Coach Brigman turned to leave. A horrible feeling spread through my body. Couldn't Coach see that Jim was up to no good?

"Oh, wait." I heard Coach stop in his tracks. "Are you the uncle that Griff was telling me about?"

Jim swung around and nodded.

"You must be so proud of him."

What was Coach doing?

"Yeah, he's my favorite nephew. Anyways—"

"Uncle Jim, right?"

"Yeah."

Coach Brigman stepped in front of Jim. "Let him go."

"I'll have him back in two minutes," Jim said.

"Yeah, let him go!" Carson held out his phone and hit Record.

"You're making a huge mistake," Jim said.

Coach Santos and Coach McKay joined us.

When I tried again to break free, Jim released me. He clenched his fist and swung, missing Coach Brigman. All three coaches did their best to restrain Jim.

"You getting this?" I asked Carson.

Jim looked at Carson, who had his cell phone aimed at him.

"Every bit."

Having more muscle than all three coaches combined, Jim managed to get free. He covered his face and took off.

"Let him go," Coach Brigman said. He turned to me. "You okay?"

I nodded. "Thank you."

"He's going to get away," Carson said.

"I don't know about that," I said. "He's got a golf bag full of drugs and money at the club. And I might have reported it to my boss."

Carson high-fived me.

"Should we get back to baseball?" Coach Brigman asked.

I shook off the numbness in my arm. I headed toward the home-run derby and started to stretch.

"You okay, Griff?"

"Yeah, I think so."

I turned to see my dad with a huge grin on his face. "So, looks like my son's going to be playing for the Hurricanes next year!"

I smiled back. "Hope so."

"Hope? Trust me, you're a guarantee."

I took a high five from him, glad he was excited for me.

Carson jogged to a stop. "Hi, Uncle Ted."

"How you doing, Carson?"

"Good."

"Don't let me stop you boys. I'll be in the stands."

Carson hit first, smoking line drives, one after the other. After his ten pitches he was all smiles.

"Looks like you were never gone."

"Can't tell you how good that felt. Thanks, coz."

"What did I do?"

"Griff, you cleared my name, got me back on the Sharks..."

"Oh, that. You're welcome."

Carson laughed and handed me the bat. "You're up."

I took the bat and stepped in front of the pitching machine. My eye was on the ball, but my mind was reeling with the events of the last few days. I took a deep breath. With this whole Wade thing taken care of, I could focus on doing my best. Maybe even lead this team to the playoffs.

The first ball came in high, and I smacked it over second base. I sent the next pitch way up into the outfield. My next hit had a nice arc and dropped deep over first base. Number four could've been better, but I was riding high. It felt great to have such a heavy weight lifted off my shoulders. Five, six and seven were hit low and hard. In a game, they all would've gotten me on base. Eight came in low, and I stretched for it. It was a line drive and I could've taken somebody's head off with it. I swung hard at the ninth ball. It had legs but started to drift foul. The tenth didn't stand a chance. I got all of it, finding its sweet spot. Maybe lifting all those golf bags at the club was paying off.

I was surprised when I saw it going for the fence. I lifted my bat into the air and watched as the ball carried over and landed in Lake Wade.

Acknowledgments

Southwest Florida, with its endless beaches, golf courses and relaxed atmosphere, has been my home away from home for many winters. My family has always allowed me time to explore and piece together scenes and plots for my stories. Their support continues to be invaluable.

To Amy Collins, my editor, who helped me to sharpen the characters, boost the conflicts and flesh out the themes. Thank you.

To the Orca team, thank you for supporting the development of novels that are high-interest, engaging, and fun to read and write.

Steven Barwin is a middle-school teacher in Toronto, Ontario. He is the author of *Hurricane Heat* in the Orca Sports series and several Lorimer Sports Stories novels, including *Fadeaway, Rock Dogs, SK8ER* and *Icebreaker*, which was chosen as a Canadian Children's Book Centre Best Books for Kids and Teens selection. For more information, visit www.stevenbarwin.com.

Titles in the Series

orca sports

orca sports

For more information on all the books
in the Orca Sports series, please visit
www.orcabook.com.